William Shakespeare's A Midsummer Night's Dream: A Retelling in Prose

David Bruce

Published by David Bruce, 2022.

WILLIAM SHAKESPEARE'S A MIDSUMMER NIGHT'S DREAM: A RETELLING IN PROSE

First edition. July 27, 2022.

Copyright © 2022 David Bruce.

ISBN: 979-8201062316

Written by David Bruce.

Table of Contents

Dedication

Dedicated to My Sister Brenda

Brenda wrote, "During COVID and when visitors were restricted from visiting their loved one in the assisted-living facility I worked at, a patient mentioned to me how much she liked spaghetti during a late-night conversation we had. She was a night owl like me. Her name was Dee. I called her "Gerdy." Then she would say, "Dirty Gerdy," and we'd laugh. Anyway, on my way to work I bought two spaghetti meals from Olive Garden. I left for work early that night. I went to work, set up outlet dinners in the dining room, went to her room and wheeled her down to the dining room where we had dinner together. At that time, the residents weren't leaving their room and had their meals alone in their room. It was nighttime and everyone was already in bed, so I didn't see a problem. She was so grateful and had enough food for three more meals. It was such a simple gesture, but during that time it meant so much to her and for me."

Brenda once bought a newspaper at a gas station on Thanksgiving and tipped the female employee $5, and the employee cried.

Brenda wrote, "I do remember that. I also remember when George tipped a TeeJays waitress $100, and she cried. Our family does a lot of good deeds all the time: I unload people's grocery carts when the people are in those electric scooters. If they are alone with a few groceries, I'll leave cash for the cashier to pay for the groceries. I've had a lot of good deeds done to me when I didn't have a lot of money. It feels good to pay it forward."

She added, "I just have one more thing to add and then I'm done. I've had a lot of people in my life do good deeds for me when I was at a low point on my life. I was at a low point for a very long time. David, you know what you've done for me, and I can never thank you enough. Martha paid for antibiotics for me when I had strep throat and didn't have money. Rosa bought me groceries. Carla has done so much, and she had us over for Easter just after Chad died. When I say US, I mean all of my kids. She was so sick and ended up at the Emergency Room that same night. Frank gave me a car. And George buys my gas for me whenever he's in Florida. And Mom and Dad were good people. I had a lot of good influences in my life that made me be a good person. At least I hope I'm a good person. I try to be someone Mom and Dad would be proud of."

***

The doing of good deeds is important. As a free person, you can choose to live your life as a good person or as a bad person. To be a good person, do good deeds. To be a bad person, do bad deeds. If you do good deeds, you will become good. If you do bad deeds, you will become bad. To become the person you want to be, act as if you already are that kind of person. Each of us chooses what kind of person we will become. To become a good person, do the things a good person does. To become a bad person, do the things a bad person does. The opportunity to take action to become the kind of person you want to be is yours.

Educate Yourself
Read Like A Wolf Eats
Be Excellent to Each Other
Books Then, Books Now, Books Forever

***

In this retelling, as in all my retellings, I have tried to make the work of literature accessible to modern readers who may lack some of the knowledge about mythology, religion, and history that the literary work's contemporary audience had.

Do you know a language other than English? If you do, I give you permission to translate this book, copyright your translation, publish or self-publish it, and keep all the royalties for yourself. (Do give me credit, of course, for the original retelling.)

I would like to see my retellings of classic literature used in schools, so I give permission to the country of Finland (and all other countries) to give copies of this book to all students forever. I also give permission to the state of Texas (and all other states) to give copies of this book to all students forever. I also give permission to all teachers to give copies of this book to all students forever.

Teachers need not actually teach my retellings. Teachers are welcome to give students copies of my eBooks as background material. For example, if they are teaching Homer's *Iliad* and *Odyssey*, teachers are welcome to give students copies of my *Virgil's* Aeneid: *A Retelling in Prose* and tell students, "Here's another ancient epic you may want to read in your spare time."

PREFACE

• Shakespeare's comic target in this play is love and the crazy things it makes us do. For example, when you are confronted with two individuals who are alike in almost every way, love can make you hate one individual while you fall in love with the other. Love can also make you fall in love with an ass — someone who is unsuited to you in every way. Theseus falls in love with Hippolyta, Queen of the Amazons, a society of women who completely rejected men and were believed to mate with men and then kill them and who were thought to kill any male babies born to them.

• Shakespeare deals with the nonrational in this play. Some things are rational, such as mathematics and logic. Other things are irrational, such as putting your hand in a blender and turning it on just to see what it feels like. The realm of the nonrational is the realm of beauty, poetry, laughter, dance, sex, and love. Comedy is nonrational. The arts connect the world of the rational and the nonrational. Much intelligence goes into producing art, but much art explores the world of the nonrational.

• Love is nonrational. Suppose you are confronted with two individuals who are basically alike in beauty, form, character, and personality, but one individual is rich and the other individual is poor. Reason would tell you to fall in love with the rich individual, but you may fall in love with the poor individual.

• The world of the nonrational appears to be more powerful than the world of the rational. Theseus is a very rational man, but despite his best intentions, he cannot help breaking out into laughter at the bad acting and bad play of the craftsmen. And, of course, he falls in love with an Amazon.

- The fairies inhabit the world of the nonrational. They speak a dazzling variety of poetry, and they sing and dance. Puck likes to play jokes on people.

- The word "irrational" means completely opposed to reason. An insane person who believes that two plus three equals four is irrational. Irrationality plays no part in *A Midsummer Night's Dream*, which is about the rational, the nonrational, and some of the places they intersect.

CAST OF CHARACTERS

THESEUS, Duke of Athens
EGEUS, father to Hermia
LYSANDER, in love with Hermia
DEMETRIUS, in love with Hermia
PHILOSTRATE, Master of the Revels to Theseus
QUINCE, a carpenter
SNUG, a joiner, aka furniture-maker
BOTTOM, a weaver
FLUTE, a bellows-mender
SNOUT, a tinker
STARVELING, a tailor
HIPPOLYTA, Queen of the Amazons, bethrothed to Theseus
HERMIA, daughter to Egeus, in love with Lysander
HELENA, in love with Demetrius
OBERON, King of the Fairies
TITANIA, Queen of the Fairies
PUCK, or ROBIN GOODFELLOW, fairy
PEASEBLOSSOM, fairy
COBWEB, fairy
MOTH, fairy
MUSTARDSEED, fairy
PROLOGUE, PYRAMUS, THISBY, WALL, MOONSHINE, LION are presented by QUINCE, BOTTOM, FLUTE, SNOUT, STARVELING, and SNUG
Other Fairies attending their King and Queen
Attendants on Theseus and Hippolyta

CHAPTER 1

In his palace, Duke Theseus of Athens was talking with Hippolyta, Queen of the Amazons, whom he had defeated in battle, fallen in love with, and was soon to marry.

Theseus said to Hippolyta, "Our wedding day is drawing near. Four happy days will bring in the new Moon, but how slowly the old Moon wanes! She prevents what I want most. She is like a stepmother or a widow who lives on a young man's inheritance when the young man wants to spend, spend, spend."

"Four days will quickly become four nights," Hippolyta replied. "We will quickly dream away the four nights. And then the Moon, resembling a silver bow newly bent in heaven, shall behold the night of our wedding."

Theseus said to Philostrate, his Master of the Revels, aka Director of Entertainments, "Go, Philostrate, encourage the Athenian youth to be merry. Awake the pert and nimble spirit of mirth. Let melancholy be reserved only for funerals. Melancholy, a pale companion, must not be present at our celebration."

Philostrate left to carry out Theseus' orders.

Theseus said, "Hippolyta, I wooed you with my sword, and I won your love, despite my doing you injuries, but I will wed you in another key, with pomp, with triumph, and with revelry."

But Theseus was the Duke of Athens, and he had duties to attend to. Egeus, the father of Hermia, walked into the room with his daughter and the two young men who loved her.

Egeus started well with a greeting to Theseus: "Happy be Theseus, our renowned duke!"

Theseus, who knew Egeus, a respected citizen of Athens and a member of its aristocracy, well, replied, "Thanks, good Egeus. What is new with you?"

"I have a problem," Egeus replied. "Full of vexation come I, with a complaint about my child, my daughter Hermia."

Egeus said, "Stand forth, Demetrius."

Demetrius came forward.

Egeus said to Theseus, "My noble lord, this man has my consent to marry my daughter, Hermia."

Egeus said, "Stand forth, Lysander."

Lysander came forward.

Egeus said to Theseus, "My gracious duke, this man has bewitched the bosom of my child."

To Lysander, Egeus angrily said, "You, you, Lysander, you have given Hermia rhymes and love poetry, and you have exchanged love-tokens with my daughter. You have by Moonlight at her window sung, with your feigning voice singing verses of feigning love. You have made her fancy you with locks of your hair, rings, gaudy toys, trinkets, knickknacks, trifles, nosegays, and sweetmeats. All of these things can strongly influence an impressionable and inexperienced young woman. With cunning you have stolen my daughter's heart. You have turned her obedience, which is due to me, into stubborn harshness. Because of you, Lysander, Hermia will not consent to marry Demetrius."

To Theseus, Egeus said, "Therefore, my gracious Duke, I want you to enforce the ancient privilege of fathers in Athens. That privilege is my right to dispose of my daughter as I wish. And that will be either to this gentleman, Demetrius, or to her death. This is in accordance with our Athenian law."

Theseus wanted daughters to obey their fathers. He said, "What do you say, Hermia? Fair maiden, to you your father should be as a god. He is your parent and so gave you your life. It is as if you are his figure that he sculpted in wax. He can either leave the figure alone or disfigure it as he wishes."

Theseus paused, and then he said, "Demetrius is a worthy gentleman."

"So is Lysander," Hermia replied, hotly.

"In himself he is," Theseus said, "but he lacks your father's approval, and therefore Demetrius must be considered the worthier of the two young men."

Hermia said, "I wish that my father looked at Demetrius and Lysander with my eyes."

"No," Theseus said. "Instead, you must look at Demetrius and Lysander with your father's eyes."

Despite being angry, Hermia was polite. She said to Theseus, "Please pardon me. I know not by what power I am made bold, and I worry that I may compromise my reputation for modesty when I plead my thoughts in your presence. But please tell me what is the worst that can happen to me if I refuse to wed Demetrius."

Theseus thought, *The law of Athens says that Hermia must die if she disobeys her father and refuses to wed Demetrius, but the law is too harsh.*

He told Hermia, "You must either be executed or become a nun and remain a virgin forever. Therefore, fair Hermia, think carefully. You are young. You feel passion. Think whether, if you do not obey your father and do not marry Demetrius, you can endure wearing the habit of a nun and be caged forever in a shady cloister. Can you live as a barren, virgin sister all your life and chant hymns to the cold, fruitless Moon? Nuns are three times blessed because they master their passion, and their maiden pilgrimage is rewarded in Heaven. But a married woman is happier on Earth and does not lack a man. She is like a rose whose essence is distilled into perfume and brings happiness. She is unlike a rose that grows, lives, and dies alone on a branch and is never enjoyed."

"I prefer to grow, live, and die alone on a branch rather than marry someone whom I do not love," Hermia said. "I prefer to remain single rather than give my virginity to someone whom I do not love."

"Take some time to think this matter over, Hermia," Theseus said. "By the next new Moon — when Hippolyta and I shall wed and be one forever — you will give me your final answer. At that time, you will either die because of your disobedience to the will of your father, or you will marry Demetrius, or you will become a nun and remain a virgin forever."

Demetrius said, "Yield to your father's will, Hermia, and marry me. And, Lysander, stop pursuing Hermia and allow her to marry me."

Lysander replied, "You have her father's love, Demetrius, so let me have Hermia's. If you want to marry someone, marry Hermia's father."

"Scornful Lysander!" Egeus said. "True, Demetrius does have my love. And whatever is mine my love shall give to him. Hermia is my daughter, and I do give her to Demetrius."

Lysander replied, "Egeus, my family is as good as the family of Demetrius. I have as much wealth as Demetrius. I love Hermia more than he does. My prospects are as good as those of Demetrius, if not better. And what is more important than anything that I have said so far is that Hermia loves me, not Demetrius. So why shouldn't Hermia and I marry?"

He added, "What's more — and I say this to Demetrius' face — he pursued Helena, the daughter of Nedar, and he won her heart. Helena loves him. She loves him, devoutly loves him, loves him to the point of idolatry. She loves Demetrius, this morally stained man who is unfaithful to those who love him."

Theseus said, "I must confess that I have heard that Demetrius pursued Helena and that she loves him. I have been busy with my own personal affairs and forgot about it; otherwise, I would have spoken to him about it. Still, that does not change the law. Demetrius and Egeus, both of you come with me. I want to talk to both of you. In the meantime, Hermia, make up your mind to obey your father and marry Demetrius, or else the law of Athens — which I can by no means extenuate — will either sentence you to death or to a single life in perpetuity."

Theseus then said, "Come, my Hippolyta."

Hippolyta had listened to the young lovers and did not look happy about Theseus' ruling. Theseus noticed this and asked her, "Is something wrong?" She turned her back on him and did not answer him.

Theseus turned to Demetrius and Egeus and said, "Come with me. I must employ you in some business related to our wedding and also talk to you about some business of your own."

"With duty and desire, we follow you," Egeus replied.

All except Lysander and Hermia left the room.

"How are you, my love?" Lysander said, "Why is your cheek so pale? Why do the roses there fade so fast?"

"Perhaps because of lack of rain," Hermia replied. "But I can well water the roses in my cheeks with my tears."

"From everything that I have ever read or heard from tale or history, the course of true love never did run smooth," Lysander said. "Either the lovers were different in family…"

"Too high a class to be in love with someone from a lower class."

"Or else the lovers were mismatched in age."

"Too old to be engaged to young."

"Or else the marriage match was to be arranged by relatives."

"Oh, Hell! To choose a lover by another's eyes."

"Or," Lysander said, "if there were a sympathy in choice, then war, death, or sickness did lay siege to it, making it as momentary as a sound, as swift as a shadow, as short as a dream, as brief as the lightning in the blackened night, that, in a flash, reveals both Heaven and Earth, and before a man has time to say 'Behold!' the jaws of darkness do devour it. So quickly do bright things that are full of life come to ruin."

"Since true lovers have always been opposed in their love, such opposition must be a rule of fate and destiny — and therefore, since our love is opposed, our love must be true,"

Hermia said. "Let us then be perseverant and enduring as we confront our trial because the trial we face is customary for true lovers. Opposition is as necessary to true love as are thoughts and dreams and sighs and wishes and tears. All of these things accompany true love."

"You speak truly," Lysander said. "Therefore, listen to me, Hermia. I have a widowed aunt. She is a dowager of great fortune, and she has no children. Her house is twenty or so miles away from Athens, and she considers me her only son. If we go to her, Hermia, we can be married — the sharp Athenian law does not reach as far as her house. So if you love me, sneak out of your father's house tomorrow night, and go into the forest outside Athens, where once I met you and Helena to celebrate the first of May. I will wait there for you."

"My good Lysander!" Hermia said. "I swear to you, by Cupid's strongest bow, by his best arrow with the love-causing golden arrowhead, by the simplicity of Venus' sacred doves, by that which unites souls and prospers loves, and by that fire that burned Dido, the Queen of Carthage, when the unfaithful Trojan Aeneas sailed away from her, by all the vows that ever men have broken, in number more than women have ever spoken, in that same place that you have mentioned, tomorrow truly will I meet with you."

"Keep your promise, love," Lysander said. He looked up and said, "Look, here comes Helena."

Hermia said, "God bless you, fair Helena! Where are you going?"

"Call you me fair?" Helena said. "That fair again unsay. Demetrius loves your beauty, not my beauty. Oh, happy fair! Your eyes are as bright as the stars that guide sailors at night.

The sweet sound of your voice is more beautiful than that of a morning lark to a shepherd's ear. When wheat is green, when hawthorn buds appear in the spring, lovesickness is contagious. I wish that appearance and attributes were also contagious. If they were so, I would do my best to catch your appearance and attributes, Hermia, before I leave. My ear would catch your voice, my eye would catch your eye, my tongue would catch your tongue's sweet melody. If I owned all the world, I would give it all to you if only I could be transformed into you and so be loved by Demetrius. Please, teach me how you look, and with what art you sway the motion of Demetrius' heart."

"I frown upon Demetrius, yet he loves me still," Hermia said.

"I wish that your frowns would teach my smiles how to make Demetrius love me!"

"I give him curses, yet he gives me love."

"I wish that my prayers could cause such affection for me in Demetrius!"

"The more I hate him, the more he follows me.

"The more I love him, the more he hates me."

"His folly, Helena, is no fault of mine."

"No fault, but your beauty — I wish that fault were mine!"

"Take comfort," Hermia said. "Demetrius no more shall see my face; Lysander and myself will flee from this place. Before I did Lysander see, Athens did seem a paradise to me, but such graces in my love do dwell, that Lysander has turned a Heaven into a Hell! If I can't marry Lysander in Athens, then Athens is a Hell to me."

Lysander said, "Helena, to you our minds we will unfold. Tomorrow night, when the Moon beholds her silver visage in the watery mirrors of pools and lakes, and dews with liquid pearl the bladed grass, a time that conceals the flights of lovers, we plan to pass through Athens' gates."

"And in the wood," Hermia said, "where often you and I upon pale primrose-beds were accustomed to lie, emptying our bosoms of their sweet secrets to each other, there my Lysander and I shall meet, and thence from Athens turn away our eyes, to seek new friends and the company of strangers. Farewell, sweet playmate. Pray for us, and may good luck give you your Demetrius! Keep your word to me, Lysander. We must now separate and starve our sight of lovers' food until we meet in the forest tomorrow at deep midnight."

"I will keep my word to you, my Hermia."

Hermia departed.

Lysander said, "Helena, *adieu*. As you on him, may Demetrius dote on you!"

Lysander departed.

Helena said to herself, "How much happier than other people can some people be! For example, Hermia is much happier than me. Throughout Athens I am thought to be as beautiful as she. But so what? Demetrius does not think it so. He will not know what all but he do know. He wanders around, infatuated with Hermia's eyes. I also wander around, admiring Demetrius' qualities. Things base and vile, having no good quality, love can make appear to have form and dignity. Love looks not with the eyes, but with the heart, and that is why in art blindfolds make winged Cupid blind. Love has nothing to do with reason — the wings and blind eyes of Cupid symbolize the unheedy haste of lovers. That is why

Cupid is said to be a child — because in choice he is so often beguiled.

"Many waggish boys in their games lie and falsely swear, and likewise male lovers perjure themselves everywhere. For before Demetrius looked at and loved Hermia's eyes, he swore many oaths that he loved only mine. His protestations of his love for me rained down like hail, but when this hail felt some heat from Hermia, his protestations of love dissolved, and showers of his oaths did melt. I will go tell him of fair Hermia's flight, and then to the forest will he pursue her tomorrow night. If for this information he tells me thanks, it is a dear expense for me, but herein mean I to enrich my pain: to have his sight thither and back again — if all goes well tomorrow night, Demetrius will stop looking at Hermia and instead will look again at me."

— 1.2 —

A number of craftsmen of Athens were meeting in the house of Peter Quince the carpenter: Nick Bottom the weaver, Francis Flute the bellows-mender, Tom Snout the tinker, Robin Starveling the tailor, and Snug the joiner, aka furniture-maker.

Quince asked, "Is all our company here?"

Bottom replied, "You were best to call them generally, man by man, according to the written list."

Generally? Quince thought. *Bottom means individually. He is a good man and a good friend, but he sometimes mixes up his words.*

"Here is a list of every man's name," Quince said, "who is thought fit, through all of Athens, to play in our interlude, or brief play, before the Duke and the Duchess on the night of their wedding day."

"First, good Peter Quince," Bottom said, "say what the play is about, and then read the names of the actors, and so come to a conclusion."

Quince said, "That's a good idea. Our play is titled 'The Most Lamentable Comedy, and Most Cruel Death of Pyramus and Thisby.'"

"I am sure that it is a very good piece of work, and a merry piece of work," Bottom said, "Now, good Peter Quince, call forth your actors by the scroll. Fellow actors, gather around him."

"Answer as I call your name," Quince said. "Nick Bottom, the weaver."

"Present," Bottom said. "Name the part that I will play, Quince, and proceed."

"You, Nick Bottom, will play Pyramus."

"What is the part of Pyramus, Quince? Is he a lover, or a tyrant?"

"He is a lover who kills himself most gallantly for love."

"That will require an actor who is capable of crying and of making the audience cry tears of sorrow," Bottom said. "If I perform the part, let the audience be careful not to injure their eyes with their crying because I will move storms — I will arouse pity in the audience."

He paused, and then he said, "And yet I would prefer to play a tyrant. I could play the role of Ercles exceptionally well."

Ercles? Quince thought. *Oh, Bottom means Hercules.*

"I could rant admirably," Bottom continued. "I could bring the house down and make the audience applaud. I will show you — listen:

"The raging rocks
"And shivering shocks
"Shall break the locks
"Of prison gates;
"And Phibbus' car
"Shall shine from afar
"And make and mar
"The foolish Fates."

That was excellent, Quince thought. *I wish I could write that well. I also wish that Bottom would say Phoebus' car, so that any listeners would understand that he is talking about the Sun-chariot of Phoebus Apollo.*

Bottom, a man of enthusiasm, enthusiastically approved of his ham acting: "That was lofty!"

He continued, "Now name the rest of the players, but that is how I would play a role like Ercles. Of course, the role of a lover is more condoling — it requires expressions of grief."

Quince resumed the roll call and role call of names:

"Francis Flute, the bellows-mender."

"Here, Peter Quince," Flute responded.

"Flute, you must play the role of Thisby."

"Who is Thisby? A wandering knight?"

"She is the lady whom Pyramus loves."

"Please, no," Flute said. "Let me not play a woman: I am growing a beard."

"That doesn't matter," Quince said. "You shall play it in a mask, and you will speak as softly and lady-like as you can."

"Since Thisby's face is hidden," Bottom said, "let me play Thisby, too. I'll speak in a monstrous little voice when I play her so people will know that I am not still playing Pyramus. Listen."

In a deep voice, Bottom declaimed, "Thisne! Thisne!"

Then in a falsetto voice, he declaimed, "Ah, Pyramus, lover dear. I am your Thisby, dear. I am your dear Thisby."

Quince said, sternly, "No, no. You must play Pyramus, and Flute must play Thisby."

Disappointed, Bottom said, "Well, proceed."

Quince read the next name on his list: "Robin Starveling, the tailor."

"Here I am, Peter Quince."

"Robin Starveling, you must play Thisby's mother."

Quince read the next name on his list: "Tom Snout, the tinker."

"Here I am, Peter Quince."

"You must play Pyramus' father, and I will play Thisby's father. One role is left. Snug the furniture-maker, you must take the part of the lion. Here, I hope, is a well-cast play."

"Have you written down the lion's part?" Snug asked. "If you have, please give it to me because I am slow of study."

"There is no need to write down the lion's part," Quince said, "because it consists of nothing but roaring."

Bottom sensed an opportunity: "Let me play the part of the lion, too. I will roar in such a way that I will do any man's heart good to hear me; I will roar in such a way that I will make the Duke say, 'Let him roar again! Let him roar again!'"

"But if you roar too ferociously," Quince objected, "you would frighten the Duchess and the ladies. They would scream, and the Duke would hang us all."

All the craftsmen agreed: "That would be enough to hang us, every mother's son."

"I grant you, friends," Bottom said, "that if any of us should frighten the ladies out of their wits, we would all be hanged, but I will aggravate my voice so that I will roar as gently as any sucking dove or nightingale roars."

There Bottom goes again, Quince thought. *He is still trying to magnify his time on stage, and still mixing up his words — he said "aggravate" when he meant to say "moderate." And "sucking" — or "suckling" — is not a word that describes a dove.*

Quince said to Bottom, "You can play no part but the part of Pyramus because Pyramus is a sweet-faced man. He is a proper man, as proper and handsome a man as anyone can see on a summer's day. He is a most lovely gentleman-like man. Therefore, you are the man who must play the role of Pyramus."

Flattered, Bottom said, "Well, I will undertake it. What beard will be best for me to play the role in?"

"You may play the role in whichever beard you prefer," Quince replied.

"I will wear either a straw-colored beard, an orange-tawny beard, a red beard, or a yellow beard that is the color of a French crown — a gold coin."

Quince joked, "Some of your French crowns have no hair at all because of the French disease: syphilis. In that case, you will have to play the part bald."

He gave each actor a sheet of paper and said, "Here are written copies of your parts for all of you to study. I entreat you, request you, and desire you to have memorized them by tomorrow night. At that time, we will meet in the forest outside of Athens. By Moonlight, we will rehearse our play. It is best to rehearse in the forest because if we rehearse in town, people will gather around and bother us, and everyone will know what we are doing. In the meantime, I will make up a list of the props that we will need for our play. Please be sure to show up tomorrow night."

Bottom replied, "We will meet you then at wherever you want; and there we may rehearse most obscenely and courageously. Take pains and study your parts carefully, everyone. We want the play to be perfect. *Adieu*."

"Then it is settled," Quince said. "We will meet at the Duke's oak tomorrow night."

"Hold, or cut bow-strings," Bottom said. "Fish, or cut bait. Poop, or get off the pot. Be there, or be square. You know what I mean. See you tomorrow night."

CHAPTER 2

— 2.1 —

In the forest near Athens, a fairy met Puck.

"How now, spirit! Whither wander you?" Puck inquired.

The fairy replied, "Over hill, over dale, through bush, through brier, over park, in light so pale, through flood, through fire, I do wander everywhere, swifter than the Moon's sphere; and I serve Titania, the fairy Queen — I dance for her upon the green. The cowslips tall her bodyguards be. In their gold coats, spots you see — those be rubies, fairy favors, and in those spots live their savors. I must go and seek some dewdrops here and hang a pearl in every cowslip's ear. Farewell, rustic spirit. I must go — and how! Our Queen and all her elves will come here now."

Puck replied, "Oberon our King does keep his revels here tonight: Take heed our Queen come not within his sight. For Oberon is very fierce and angry because Titania has a new attendant: a lovely boy, stolen from an Indian King. She has never had so sweet a changeling. Jealous Oberon would make the child a knight of his train of followers, so the child can walk through the forests wild. But Titania withholds the beloved boy, crowns him with flowers and makes him all her joy. Now Oberon and Titania never meet in grove or green, by fountain clear, or in spangled starlight sheen. Instead, they quarrel, and all their elves do fear and creep into acorn-cups and hide them there."

The fairy recognized Puck, a celebrity in Fairyland: "Either I mistake your shape and form quite, or else you are that shrewd and knavish sprite called Robin Goodfellow. Aren't you he who frightens the maidens of the villagery, skims the cream from milk, and sometimes makes the breathless housewife grind and churn but make no flour and no butter that will for her money earn? Aren't you he who sometimes makes the beer to bear no froth and misleads night-wanderers, laughing at them when they are lost? Some call you Hobgoblin, and others call you Puck, and those you befriend will have good luck. Aren't you that Puck?"

"You speak aright," Puck replied. "I am that merry wanderer of the night. I jest to Oberon and make him smile, and sometimes I a fat and bean-fed horse beguile when I neigh as if I were a filly foal. Sometimes I hide in a gossip's bowl as if I were a roasted crabapple, and when she drinks, against her lips I bob and on her withered dewlap pour the ale. The wisest aunt, telling the saddest tale, sometimes for a three-foot stool mistakes me. When she tries to sit on me, then slip I from her bum, and down topples she, and she falls on the floor roughly and after she falls she coughs. Then her friends hold their hips and laugh and sneeze and swear — a merrier hour was never spent there. But make room, fairy — here comes Oberon!"

"And here comes Titania, my mistress. I wish that Oberon were gone!"

The Fairy King and Queen appeared with many attendants.

"Ill met by Moonlight, proud Titania," Oberon said.

"What, jealous Oberon, are you here? Fairies, let us leave at once. I have sworn never again to be in Oberon's bed or in his presence."

"Stay here, rash wanton," Oberon said. "Isn't it true that I am your husband?"

"Then I must be your wife," Titania replied, "but I know of your affairs. I know when you have stolen away from Fairyland, and in the shape of a mortal lover sat all day, playing on a homemade flute and singing verses of love to an amorous mortal lover. Why are you here, recently returned from the farthest mountain range of India? You must be here because Hippolyta, the swaggering Amazon, your boot-wearing mistress and your warrior love, to Theseus is going to be married, and you have come to give their bed joy and prosperity."

"For shame, Titania," Oberon replied. "How can you criticize my love for Hippolyta when I know about your love for Theseus? Haven't you protected him from the consequences of his affairs? Didn't you lead him through the glimmering night when he abandoned Perigenia, whom he had kidnapped and seduced? And didn't you help him when he seduced and abandoned Aegles, Ariadne, and Antiopa? Theseus has been quite the lover boy, and without fairy help, he would have paid for his seductions and not felt joy!"

"These are the lies of jealousy," Titania replied. "Ever since the beginning of midsummer, each time we have met, whether on hill or in dale, forest, or meadow, by paved fountain or by brook banked with growing rushes, or on the beaches of the sea, to dance our ringlets to the whistling winds, you have disturbed our dances with your quarrels."

Titania added, "Because you and I, the King and Queen of Fairyland, are quarreling, the winds, tired of singing to us in vain, in revenge have sucked up from the sea noxious waters, which have fallen as rain in the land and have made every petty river so grand and so proud that they have overflowed their banks. Because of our quarrel, crops will not grow — the ox has pulled in vain the plow, the farmer has nothing for his sweat to show, and the green corn dies before the cob grows a silky beard. In the flooded fields stand pens empty of sheep, and crows grow fat from feasting on the dead flock's meat. Covered with mud are football fields, and paths grow faint with disuse that were by lovers formerly filled."

Titania continued, "Because of our quarrel, the natural seasons are confused. Human mortals lack their winters, a season that has its pleasures. No night is blessed with hymn or carol, and the Moon, the governess of floods, pale in her anger, washes all the air, causing colds and rheumatic diseases. The disturbance in the natural order caused by our quarrel has altered the seasons. Hoary-headed frost coats the crimson roses, and the mocking crown of Old Man Winter is a sweet-smelling wreath of summer buds. Spring, summer, autumn, and winter are all mixed up, and the amazed world no longer knows which is when. All of these evils come from our quarrel — we are their parents and origin."

"You can easily fix everything," Oberon replied, "Why should you argue with me? I do but beg a little changeling boy, my servant to be. Give him to me."

"That won't happen," Titania said. "Not all of Fairyland would I take for the boy. His mother was a priestess of my order, and, in the spiced Indian air, by night, very often has given me joy as she talked with me and sat with me on the sea's yellow sands, watching the traders sailing on the ocean. We have laughed as we watched the ships' sails conceive and grow pregnant by the wanton wind. She — pregnant with the child, and walking with a pretty swimming gait — imitated the big-bellied sails. She sailed upon the land, got for me small gifts, and returned again, as if she had returned from a voyage, rich with merchandise. Unfortunately, she, being mortal, died giving birth to that boy; for her sake I will bring up her boy, and for her sake I will not part from him."

"How long within this forest do you intend to stay?" Oberon asked.

"Probably until after Theseus' wedding day," Titania replied. If you will peacefully dance in our circles and see our Moonlit revels, you are welcome to come with us. If you are not willing to be peaceful, then shun me, and I will shun your haunts."

"Give me that boy, and I will happily go with you."

"I will not give you the boy even if you give me your fairy kingdom," Titania replied. "He stays with me and my followers. Fairies, away! Oberon and I will loudly quarrel, if I longer stay."

Titania and her fairies departed.

Oberon said to himself, "Well, go your way, but you shall not depart from this forest until after I torment you for not giving me that boy."

He said louder, "My dear Puck, come here. Do you remember when once I sat upon a promontory, and heard a mermaid on a dolphin's back singing such a sweet and harmonious song that the high waves of the sea calmed and stars fell out of the sky to come closer to hear the sea-maiden sing?"

"I remember."

"That was the time I — but not you — saw Cupid, armed with arrows, flying between the cold Moon and the Earth. He took aim at a virgin sitting in a throne in the West, and he shot his love-arrow smartly from his bow and it seemed as if it could pierce a hundred thousand hearts. But the Moon is ruled by the virgin goddess Diana, and the chaste beams of the silvery Moon put out the flames of young Cupid's fiery shaft, and the virgin continued to think the thoughts of a maiden and neglected to think the thoughts of a lover. I remember where the arrow of Cupid fell. It fell upon a little flower in the West. The flower used to be milky white, but now it is purple — it changed colors when hit by Cupid's arrow just as love's wound causes maidens to change colors when their beloved's name is mentioned. Maidens call that flower love-in-idleness. Fetch me that flower — I once showed it to you. The juice of that flower when squeezed onto sleeping eyelids will make a man or woman madly love the next live creature it sees. Fetch me that flower quickly — before a whale can swim three miles."

"I'll put a girdle round about the earth in forty minutes," Puck replied, and then he flew away.

Oberon said to himself, "Once I have this juice, I will wait until Titania is asleep, and then I will drip its juice onto her eyelids. The next thing she waking looks upon, be it a lion, bear, wolf, or bull, or a meddling monkey or ape, she shall pursue with the soul of love. And before I take this charm from off her sight, as I can with another herb, I will make her give up the Indian boy to me."

Oberon heard a noise, and he said to himself, "But who are coming here? I will make myself invisible, and I will overhear their conversation."

Demetrius and Helena came close to Oberon, whom they did not see.

Exasperated, Demetrius said to Helena, "I do not love you, so stop following me. Where are Lysander and fair Hermia? The one I will slay, the other has already slain me with her lack of love. You told me they had stolen away from Athens and come to this forest, and I am going nutty among these nut trees and batty among these homes for bats and wild in this wilderness, all because I cannot find Hermia. Go away, leave me, and follow me no more."

"Your attractiveness attracts me toward you," Helena replied. "The kind of love you draw from my heart is not base iron but a finer metal, for my heart is as true as steel. Only if your attractiveness stops attracting me toward you will I stop following you."

"Do I entice you?" Demetrius said. "Do I speak fair words to you? No! Instead, I in plain truth and in plain language tell you that I do not and I cannot love you."

"And even for that do I love you the more," Helena replied. "I am your cocker spaniel, I am your pet dog, and, Demetrius, the more you beat me, the more I will love you. Treat me as you treat your cocker spaniel, spurn me, strike me, neglect me, lose me. Do whatever you want to me as long as you allow me, unworthy as I am, to follow you. What worser place can I beg in your love — and yet for me it is a place of high respect — than to be treated by you as you treat your dog?"

"Be careful not to put to the test my hatred of you because I am sick when I look at you."

"And I am sick when I do not look at you," Helena replied.

"You do risk your reputation and your virginity too much, to leave the city and commit yourself into the hands of me, a man who does not love you. It is dark, we are in a deserted place, and if I were a different kind of man, I could force myself on you."

"Your goodness will protect me and prevent you from taking advantage of me," Helena said. "When I look at you, I see no night, and therefore I see no darkness. This forest is not deserted. Why? Because you are my entire world. How can anyone say that I am alone, when all the world is standing in front of me?"

"I'll run from you and hide in the thickets and leave you to the mercy of wild beasts," Demetrius said.

"The wildest of wild animals has not such a heart as you. Run whenever and wherever you will; the story of Apollo and Daphne shall be changed. In the old tale, the mortal Daphne ran from the god Apollo, who pursued her. But with you as Apollo and with me as Daphne, Apollo will flee, and Daphne will chase. The dove will pursue the eagle; the mild doe will speed to catch the tiger. A coward will pursue a fleeing brave man!"

"I will not stay around to listen to you. Either let me leave you, or be afraid that if you follow me I will do some harm to you in these woods."

Fortunately, despite making the threat, Demetrius was not the kind of man who would carry out the threat.

"You have already done harm to me in the temple, in the town, and in the field, Demetrius! You have wronged me by making me do the wooing, and you have wronged all women! Women cannot fight for love, as men may do; women should be wooed and were not made to woo. You, Demetrius, should be wooing me."

Demetrius made a motion as if to kick her and then fled.

Helena said, "I will follow you and make a Heaven of Hell, by dying at the hand of the man I love so well."

She ran after Demetrius.

Oberon had watched and heard everything, and his own marital woes made him empathize with Helena.

He said, "Fare thee well, nymph. You are of an age to be married to this young man, and before he leaves this grove, you shall flee from him and he shall seek your love."

Puck, having returned from his journey, went to Oberon, who said, "Welcome, wanderer. Do you have the flower?"

"Yes, here it is."

"Please give it to me," Oberon said. "I know a bank where the wild thyme blows, where oxlips and the nodding violet grows. It is quite over-canopied with luscious woodbine, with sweet musk-roses and with eglantine. There sleeps Titania sometimes during the night, and among all those flowers she is lulled by dances and delight. There the snake sheds its enameled skin, which is wide enough to make a garment to wrap a fairy in. With the juice of this flower, I will streak Titania's eyes, and make her mind full of lovesick fantasies."

He added, "Puck, take part of this flower and look throughout this grove for a sweet young Athenian lady who is in love with a youth who disdains her. Anoint his eyes with the juice of this flower, but do it when the next thing he sees will be the Athenian lady. You shall know the man by the Athenian clothing he is wearing. Do what I tell you to do with care, so that he will be more in love with her than she is in love with him, and know that you must meet me before the first cock crows."

"Fear not, my King, your servant shall do so."

— 2.2 —

In another part of the forest, Titania and her fairy attendants were settling in for the night.

Titania ordered, "Come and dance in a fairy ring and sing a fairy song. Then leave and attend to your duties. Some of you will kill cankerworms in the musk-rose buds, and some of you will war with bats and take their leathern wings to make my small elves coats, and some of you will keep back the clamorous owl that nightly hoots and wonders at our dainty spirits. Sing me now asleep, then attend to your work and let me rest."

The fairies sang this song:

"You spotted snakes with forked tongue,

"and thorny hedgehogs, be not seen.

"Newts and small snakes, do no wrong,

"come not near our fairy Queen.

"Nightingale, with melody,

"sing in our sweet lullaby.

"Lulla, lulla, lullaby, lulla, lulla, lullaby.

"May no harm,

"or spell or charm,

"come near our lovely lady here.

"Say good night with a lullaby.

"Weaving spiders, come not here.

"Go away, you long-legged spinners, go hence!

"Beetles black, approach not near.

"Snake and snail, do no offence.

"Nightingale, with melody,

"sing in our sweet lullaby.
"Lulla, lulla, lullaby, lulla, lulla, lullaby.
"May no harm,
"or spell or charm,
"come near our lovely lady here.
"Say good night with a lullaby."

A fairy said, "Away we go! All is well! One alone stand sentinel."

Most of the fairies departed, and the lone sentinel made a poor guard. The sentinel did not dare interfere with Oberon, King of the Fairies, and flew away when Oberon appeared.

Oberon walked to the sleeping Titania and squeezed the juice of the flower onto her eyelids and said, "Whatever you see when you wake, do it for your true love take. Love and languish for his sake. Whether it be lynx, or wildcat, or bear, or panther, or boar with bristled hair, whatever shall appear before your eyes when you do awake, you shall love it for its own sake. Whatever you see when you do wake, dear Titania, you will hold it dear, so wake when some vile thing is near."

As soon as Oberon flew away, Lysander and Hermia walked close to Titania, the sleeping fairy Queen, but they did not see her.

Lysander said to Hermia, "Fair love, you are faint from much wandering in the wood; and to say the truth, I have forgotten our way: We are lost. Let us rest here, Hermia, if you think it a good idea, and we will wait for the comfort of morning and daylight."

"Let it be done," Hermia said. "Lysander, find a place for you to make your bed, for I upon this bank will rest my head."

"One piece of ground shall serve as bed for us both," Lysander said. "We need no ground between us to waste. We will have one bed and one heart, and we will pledge to each other our lover's faith."

"No, good Lysander, Hermia replied. "For my sake, my dear, lie further away, do not lie by me so near."

"Understand what is behind my words, my sweet, and know that it is innocence!" Lysander said. "Lovers understand each other's meaning in each sentence. I mean that my heart unto yours is so knit that only one heart we can make of it, and both of us know we do love each other. So by your side let me tonight lie, for when I tell you I love you, you know I do not lie."

"Lysander, you speak very prettily, and please forgive me if you thought that I think you lied, but gentle friend, for love and courtesy lie further away. Be courteous and let there be such separation between us as may well be said becomes a virtuous bachelor and a modest maiden. So make your bed at a distance from me, and good night, sweet friend. May your love for me never alter until your life ends."

Lysander was disappointed, but he was a man who took no for an answer, so he said, "Amen, amen, to that fair prayer, say I; and may my life end when I end my love for you! Over here will I make my bed. May you sleep well where you rest your sweet head."

"May you sleep as well as I, while I take my rest in my sweet nest," Hermia replied.

Hermia and Lysander were asleep when Puck arrived and complained, "Throughout the forest have I gone, but Athenian found I none on whose eyes I might test this flower's force in causing love. All is night and silence."

Puck then caught sight of Lysander: "Who is here? Clothing of Athens he does wear. This is he, my master said, who despised the Athenian maiden."

Puck then looked at Hermia and said, "And here is the maiden, sleeping sound, on the dank and dirty ground. Pretty soul! She dares not lie near this lack-love, this kill-courtesy."

Puck went to Lysander and squeezed the juice of the flower onto his sleeping eyelids.

He then said, "Chump, upon your eyes have I thrown all the power this charm does own. When you wake, you pest, may love forbid you any more rest. So awake when I am gone, for I must go to Oberon."

Puck flew away, and immediately Demetrius and Helena ran near Lysander and Hermia and stopped.

"Stay here and run no more, even though you kill me, sweet Demetrius," Helena pleaded.

"I order you to leave and to leave me alone," Demetrius replied.

"Will you leave me in the dark? Do not so."

"Stay here, or face my anger. I alone will go," Demetrius said before crashing through the forest again.

"Oh, I am out of breath in this fond chase!" Helena said. "The more I pray, the less is my grace. Happy is Hermia, wherever she lies, for she has blessed and attractive eyes. Why are her eyes so bright? Salt tears did not make them bright. My eyes are oftener washed with salt tears than hers, and my eyes are not so bright as hers. No, no, I am as ugly as a bear. Beasts that meet me run away in fear. Therefore, I should not marvel that Demetrius runs away from me as if he were from a monster fleeing. What wicked and lying mirror made me seek to compare my eyes with Hermia's eyes that are as bright as the stars in the sky at night?"

Helena, seeing Lysander lying on the ground, said, "But who is here? Lysander! On the ground! Is he dead? Or asleep? I see no blood, no wound. Lysander, if you live, good sir, awake."

Lysander awoke and said, "And run through fire I will for your sweet sake. Radiant Helena! Now that I have awakened, I can see into your heart. Where is Demetrius? Oh, how fit a word is that vile name to perish on my sword!"

"Do not say that, Lysander; do not say that," Helena said. "So what if he loves your Hermia? It doesn't matter because Hermia still loves you. Be content with that, and leave Demetrius alone."

"Content with Hermia!" Lysander said. "No! I do repent the tedious minutes I with her have spent. Not Hermia but Helena I love. Who will not change a raven for a dove? The love a man feels is by his reason swayed, and reason says you are the worthier maiden. Things growing are not ripe until their season, so I, being young, was not until now ripe to reason. Now that I have grown up, reason becomes the leader of my will and leads me to your eyes, where I look and see love's stories written in love's richest book."

Helena was certain that Lysander was cruelly mocking her by pretending to be in love with her. She complained, "Why was I to this keen mockery born? When at your hands did I deserve this scorn? Is it not enough, young man, that I did never, no, nor never can, despite how I try, deserve a sweet look from Demetrius' eyes? Why then must you mock my insufficiency? You do me wrong, you do, by pretending to love me and me to woo. But fare you well, although I must confess I thought you were a man of true gentleness. Oh, that a lady, by one man refused, should by another therefore be ill used!"

Helena ran away from Lysander.

Lysander said, "She did not see Hermia. Hermia, sleep you here, and may you never come Lysander near! Just like a surfeit of the sweetest things, the deepest loathing to the stomach brings, or as the heresies that men do leave are hated most by those whom the heresies did deceive, so you, my surfeit and my heresy, by all be hated, but most of all by me! And, all my talents, address your love and might to honor Helen and to be her knight!"

Lysander ran after Helena.

A nightmare woke Hermia: "Help me, Lysander, help me! Do your best to pluck this crawling serpent from my breast! What a nightmare I had here! Lysander, look how I do shake with fear. I thought that a serpent was eating my heart, and you sat smiling as the serpent played his part. Lysander! Gone?"

She shouted, "Lysander! Can you hear me?"

She listened, and then she said, "You must be out of range of hearing me. Lysander, where are you? Speak, if you can hear me! Speak, my love! I almost faint with fear!"

No reply came, and Hermia said, "I know you are not near. I will go and seek you because you are my dear. I will find either my dear or my death."

CHAPTER 3

— 3.1 —

Titania, Queen of the Fairies, lay asleep near the place in the forest where the craftsmen of Athens — Bottom, Quince, Snug, Flute, Snout, and Starveling — had come to practice their play.

Bottom asked, "Are we all here?"

"Yes, we are," Quince said, "and here is a marvelous and convenient place for our rehearsal. This green patch of grass shall be our stage, and this hawthorn thicket shall be our backstage. We will rehearse our play as we will do it before the Duke."

"Peter Quince," Bottom said.

"What do you want, good friend Bottom?"

"There are things in this comedy of Pyramus and Thisby that will never please the audience. First, Pyramus must draw a sword to kill himself, which the ladies will not stand. What do you say to that?"

Snout said, "Bottom is right. The ladies will be frightened."

Starveling said, "I believe we must leave the killing out."

"No, we can leave the killing in the play," Bottom said. "I have a device that will make all well. Quince, write me a prologue, and let the prologue seem to say that we will do no harm with our swords, and that Pyramus is not killed indeed; and, for the better assurance, tell them that I, Pyramus, am not Pyramus, but Bottom the weaver. This will keep the ladies from being afraid."

"That's a good idea," Quince said. "We will have such a prologue; and it shall be written in alternating eight- and six-syllable lines."

"No," Bottom objected, "make it two more; let it be written in eight and eight."

Snout asked, "Won't the ladies be afraid of the lion?"

"I am afraid of it, I promise you," Starveling said.

"We need to think carefully about bringing a lion onstage," Bottom said. "To bring in — Heaven help us! — a lion among ladies is a most dreadful thing because there is not a more fearful wild-fowl than your lion living."

"Therefore another prologue must say that he is not a lion," Snout suggested.

Bottom considered that idea — he might be able to have more lines to recite — but he wanted his friends to get recognition, too. Therefore, he said, "No, the actor playing the lion must say his name, and half his face must be seen through the lion's neck, and he himself must speak through, saying this, or to the same defect — 'Ladies,' or 'Fair ladies' — 'I would wish you,' or 'I would request you,' or 'I would entreat you, not to fear, not to tremble. I pledge my life to protect yours. If you think I am come hither as a lion, it could mean the end of my life. No, I am not a lion; I am a man as other men are.' Then let the lion tell the ladies plainly that he is Snug the joiner."

"It shall be done," Quince said. "But there are two hard things that remain. First, how can we bring the Moonlight into a chamber? According to the story, Pyramus and Thisby meet by Moonlight."

"Does the Moon shine the night that we play our play?" Snout asked.

"A calendar, a calendar!" Bottom said. "Look in the almanac and see whether the Moon shines that night."

Quince took a book out of his pocket, turned some pages, and said, "Yes, the Moon shines that night."

"Good," Bottom said. "We can open a window, and the Moon will shine through the window."

"Yes, that will work," Quince said, "or one of us actors could come in with a bushel of thorns and a lantern, and say he comes to disfigure, or to present, the person of Moonshine."

Flute thought, *That would work. The man could be the Man in the Moon. According to an old story, a man gathered thorns for firewood on Sunday and as punishment, he was placed on the Moon to live thereafter. And interestingly, Bottom — who said "defect" when he meant "effect"— is not the only one here who sometimes misuses words. Quince talked about how one of us actors could "disfigure" the Moon when he meant that one of us could be the figure — the symbol — of the Moon. Quince also said that that actor could "present" the person of Moonshine, but he should have said, "represent." So be it. We all make mistakes.*

Quince added, "There is a second problem that we must solve. We must have a wall in the great chamber because Pyramus and Thisby, according to the story, did talk through the chink of a wall."

"We cannot bring a wall into the Duke's great chamber," Snout said. "Do you have any ideas about what we can do, Bottom?"

"Some man or other must present Wall," Bottom said, "and let him have some plaster, or some clay, or some cement to signify a wall; and let him hold his fingers like this" — Bottom made an OK sign with the fingers of his right hand — "and through that O shall Pyramus and Thisby whisper."

"If we do that, then all is well," Quince said. "Come, sit down, every mother's son, and we will rehearse our parts. Pyramus, you begin. When you have spoken your speech, enter into that thicket. That is where you should be unless you are onstage."

Puck flew near and noticed the craftsmen. He made himself invisible and walked among them, saying, "Here are Athenian craftsmen who are wearing homespun cloth of hemp. What hempen homespuns are these swaggering here, so near the bed of the fairy Queen? I see! They are rehearsing a play. I will be their audience. I will also be an actor, if I see fit."

Quince, the director as well as the author of the play, said, "Speak, Pyramus. Thisby, come forward."

Bottom, as Pyramus, said to Flute, who was playing Thisby, "Thisby, the flowers of odious savors sweet —"

Quince corrected him, "Odors, odors."

"Odors savors sweet," Bottom said, "So has your breath, my dearest Thisby dear. But hark, a voice! Stay thou but here awhile, and by and by I will to thee appear."

Bottom exited, and Puck said to himself, "He is the strangest Pyramus that I have ever seen!" Then Puck followed Bottom.

"Must I speak now?" Flute asked.

"Yes," Quince said. "Pyramus has left to see about a voice that he heard, and he is to come back again soon."

Flute recited, "Most radiant Pyramus, most lily-white of hue,

"Of color like the red rose on triumphant brier,

"Most lively juvenile and eke most lovely Jew,

"As true as truest horse that yet would never tire,

"I'll meet thee, Pyramus, at Ninny's tomb."

"Say 'Ninus' tomb.' Ninus was the founder of the ancient city Nineveh," Quince said, "but don't say that line yet. Pyramus will come back and speak, and then you will say that line to him."

Quince complained, "Why, you are speaking all your lines at once, cues and all."

Quince then called to Bottom, "Pyramus, enter. Your cue for coming onstage has been spoken — it is 'never tire.'"

Flute said, "Oh!" and then recited, "As true as truest horse that yet would never tire."

Bottom and Puck came out of the thicket. Puck had worked some magic, and Bottom now had the head of an ass, or donkey.

Bottom declaimed, "If I were handsome, Thisby, I would still be only yours."

Quince saw Bottom's ass' head and shouted, "Oh, monstrous! Oh, strange! We are haunted! Flee from here, friends! Help!"

The craftsmen, with the exception of Bottom, ran away.

Puck was happy to add to the excitement of the fleeing craftsmen, especially since it involved shape-shifting: "I'll follow you, I'll lead you roundabout, through bog, through bush, through brake, through brier. Sometimes a horse I'll be, sometimes a hound, a hog, or a headless bear, sometimes a fire; and I will neigh, and bark, and grunt, and roar, and burn, like horse, hound, hog, bear, fire, at every turn."

Bottom asked himself, "Why do they run away? They are playing a joke on me and trying to make me afraid and trying to make an ass of me."

Snout, trying to escape from one of Puck's transformations, almost ran over Bottom. He stopped long enough to say, "Oh, Bottom, you have changed! What do I see on you?"

"What do you see?" Bottom said, "You see an ass' head of your own, do you?"

Snout ran away, but Quince took his place and said, "Heaven help you, Bottom! You are translated."

Had Flute been present and unpanicked, he would have thought, *Quince meant to say "transformed."*

Bottom said to himself, "I see their knavery. They are playing a joke on me to make an ass of me. They are trying to frighten me if they can. But I will not move from this place — let them do whatever they can. I will walk up and down here, and I will sing, so that they shall hear that I am not afraid."

He sang, "*The blackbird so black of hue,*

"*With its orange-tawny bill,*

"*The song thrush with his note so true,*

"*The wren with its little trill —*"

Hearing Bottom sing, the fairy Queen Titania woke up, looked at him, and said, "What angel wakes me from my flowery bed?"

Bottom continued to sing:

"*The finch, the sparrow and the lark,*

"*The plain-song cuckoo gray,*

"*Whose note full many a man does note,*

"*And dares not answer nay —*"

Bottom thought a moment, and then he said to himself, "Why would anyone be so foolish as to answer a foolish cuckoo? The cuckoo calls a man a cuckold. A cuckold is a man whose wife cheats on him. By answering the cuckoo, the man would show that he was paying attention to what the cuckoo called out. It is as if the cuckoo were talking to him and letting him know that he is a cuckold. It is best to ignore the cuckoo so that other people think that the cuckoo is talking to some other man."

Titania said, "I beg you, gentle mortal, please sing again. My ears are much enamored of your notes, and my eyes are much enthralled by your shape. The power of your beauty moves me at first sight to say — no, to swear — that I love you."

Titania tossed her hair, pulled her shoulders back, and pushed her chest forward. She twisted her torso from right to left and back to show off her breasts from different angles, and she giggled. Suddenly, the fairy Queen was acting like a fourteen-year-old — or older — mortal girl who had found "true love."

Bottom, the most foolish of men, now said the most wise of words: "I think, lady, you have little reason to say that, and yet, to say the truth, reason and love keep little company together nowadays."

He thought, *Occasionally, I can say exactly the right words.*

Then he said, "It's a pity that some respectable neighbors will not make them friends."

He thought, *Occasionally, I can make a good jest.*

Titania said, "You are as wise as you are beautiful."

"I deny that," Bottom said, "but if I had wit enough to get out of this forest, I would have wit enough for me."

"Out of this forest, do not desire to go," Titania said. "You shall remain here, whether you want to stay or go. I am a spirit of no common rate — the summer serves me and my estate — and I do love you. Therefore, go with me. I will give you fairies to be your servants, and they shall fetch you jewels from the deep, and sing while you on pressed flowers do sleep, and I will purge your mortal body so that you shall like an airy spirit go."

Titania called some elves: "Peaseblossom! Cobweb! Mote! Mustardseed!"

Peaseblossom said, "I am ready to do your will."

Cobweb said, "So am I."

Mote said, "So am I."

Mustardseed said, "So am I."

All asked, "What do you want us to do?"

Titania replied, "Elves, be kind and courteous to this gentleman. Go with him wherever he walks, and dance for him. Feed him with apricots and dewberries, with purple grapes, green figs, and mulberries. Steal the honey bags from the bumblebees. Steal beeswax from them and use glowworms to light the wax and make candles so that my love can see to go to bed and to arise. Pluck the wings from beautiful butterflies to fan the Moonbeams from his sleeping eyes. Bow to him, and curtsey, my elves."

Peaseblossom said, "Welcome, mortal!"

Cobweb said, "Welcome!"

Mote said, "Welcome!"

Mustardseed said, "Welcome!"

"I beg your pardon, elves," Bottom said. He asked one elf, "What is your name?"

"Cobweb."

Bottom joked, "Cobwebs are used to stop the bleeding from small cuts, so if I cut my finger, I shall become better acquainted with you."

He asked another elf, "Your name, honest gentleman?"

"Peaseblossom."

Bottom joked, "Please give my regards to Mistress Squash, your mother, and to Master Peascod, your father. Good Master Peaseblossom, I shall also become better acquainted with you."

He asked another elf, "What is your name, please, sir?"

"Mustardseed."

Bottom joked, "Beef is often eaten with mustard. I promise you that your relatives have many times made my eyes water. I shall also become better acquainted with you, good Master Mustardseed."

"Be my love's servants," Titania said to the fairies. "Lead him to my bed. The Moon, I think, looks sad and tearful. And when the Moon weeps, every little flower weeps. The flowers lament chastity — either the chastity of those who want to lose it but cannot or the chastity of those who want to keep it but cannot. Tie up my love's tongue — cover his mouth — and bring him to my bed silently."

— **3.2** —

In another part of the forest, Oberon said to himself, "I wonder whether Titania has awakened, and I wonder what living thing it was that first she saw — that is the thing that she must love fiercely."

Puck flew to Oberon, who said, "Welcome back, Puck. How now, mad spirit! What night sports are going on now about this much-populated forest?"

Puck replied, "Titania with a monster is in love. Near to her secret and consecrated bower, while she was in her dull and sleeping hour, a crew of fools, ignorant craftsmen, who work in Athens, met together to rehearse a play intended for great Theseus' wedding day. The most foolish of all those actors, who played the part of Pyramus, exited the 'stage' and entered a thicket, and there I played a joke on his thick head, on which I placed an ass' head. He returned to Thisby to talk, and when his fellow actors did him spy, they scattered as do geese whom hunters stalk. At the sound of a gun, geese and jackdaws rise in the sky, and in the forest the actors did fly as they scattered and fled. Over a stump an actor fell and rolled and cried 'Murder' and called for help from Athens. Their strong fears conquered their weak minds, and they became afraid of bushes and vines, for briers and thorns at their clothing snatched, and from some actors hats and from other actors sleeves catched. I led the actors on in this distracted fear, and left foolish Pyramus transformed there. At that moment, so it came to pass, Titania woke up and loved an ass."

"This has turned out better than I could have planned," Oberon said. "But have you yet put the juice of the flower upon the Athenian's eyelids as I ordered you to do?"

"I did that while he was sleeping," Puck replied, "so that is done, too. The Athenian woman was by his side, and so, when he wakes up, by him she must be eyed."

Hermia and Demetrius ran onto the scene, and Oberon and Puck made themselves invisible.

"Here comes the Athenian man," Oberon said.

"This is the woman I saw, but I have never seen this man," Puck said.

Demetrius said, "Why do you rebuke me when I love you so? You should be this bitter to your bitter foe."

Hermia replied, "My rebuke of you is now gentle, but it can become much worse. I am afraid that you may have given me reason enough you to curse. If you have slain Lysander in his sleep, you are up to your ankles in blood, and you might as well wade into a deep ocean of blood and kill me, too."

She added, "Lysander is more faithful to me than the Sun is to the day. Would Lysander from his sleeping Hermia have stolen away? I will sooner believe that the Earth has a hole bored through it and the Moon has passed through the hole and has come out on the other side of the Earth to disrupt the tides and annoy her brother, the Sun. You must have murdered Lysander. You even look like a murderer: deadly and grim."

"The murdered should look dead and grim," Demetrius said, "and that is how I should look. Your stern cruelty has pierced me through the heart, yet you, my murderer, look as bright, as clear, as yonder Venus in her glimmering sphere."

"What do your words have to do with Lysander?" Hermia asked. "What have you done with him? Where is he? Demetrius, will you give him back to me?"

"I prefer to give his carcass to my hounds."

"Go away, dog! Go away, cur! You have driven me past the bounds of a maiden's patience! Have you murdered Lysander? If so, then from here on never be thought to be a man! Just for once, tell me the truth. Do it for my sake! Would you have been capable of even looking at him when he was awake? Did you kill him while he was asleep? How brave! Could not a poisonous snake that way behave? You are the snake who murdered Lysander. You, Demetrius, have a tongue that is more forked than that of any biting snake.”

“You are angry at the wrong person,” Demetrius said. “I am not guilty of killing Lysander. He is still alive, for all that I can tell.”

“Please tell me then that he is well.”

“And if I could, what should I get therefore?”

“The privilege never to see me more. From your hated presence I now part. See me no more, whether Lysander is dead or not.”

Hermia ran away from Demetrius.

“There is no use following her when she is in this fierce vein,” Demetrius said. “Here therefore for a while I will remain. The heaviness of my sorrow grows even heavier because I have lost sleep due to my woe. Because of my sorrow, I am owed a debt by sleep. Here for a while I will stay, and some of that debt sleep shall repay.”

Demetrius lay on the ground and slept.

“What have you done!” Oberon said to Puck. “You were mistaken quite, and you laid the love-juice on some true love’s sight. Because of your mistake, that which ensued is a true love turned false and not a false love turned true.”

“Fate is at fault, not I,” Puck said. “In this world, for every man who is faithful to his lover, a million fail, breaking oath on oath.”

“Throughout the forest, go swifter than the wind, no matter how much your path may wind, and Helena of Athens make sure you find,” Oberon ordered. “All lovesick she is and lacks good cheer; she makes sighs of love that cost her dear.

By some illusion, bring her here. I'll charm Demetrius' eyes in preparation for when she does appear."

"I go! I go! Look how I go, swifter than an arrow from a Tartar's bow."

Puck flew swiftly away.

Oberon squeezed the flower, and let the juice drip onto Demetrius' sleeping eyelids, saying, "Flower of this purple dye, hit with Cupid's arrow, make Helena the apple of his eye. When his love he do espy, let her shine as gloriously as does Venus in the sky."

Oberon then said to Demetrius, "When you awake, may Helena be by. Sincerely beg her to love you — do not lie."

Puck returned and said, "Captain of our fairy band, Helena is here at hand, and the youth, mistook by me, pleading for a lover's fee. Shall we their foolish pageant see? Lord, what fools these mortals be!"

"Stand back," Oberon said. "The noise that Helena and Lysander make will awaken Demetrius."

Delighted, Puck said, "Then will two at the same time woo one, and that will make good fun. All the things that best please me are those that happen preposterously."

Lysander and Helena walked near Demetrius.

Lysander pleaded, "Why should you think that I woo you in scorn? Tears never accompany scorn and derision. Look, when I vow that I love you, I weep; and vows so born and accompanied with tears are known to be true. How can my tears seem like scorn to you, when they are evidence that shows that I am true?"

"Your words grow trickier and trickier," Helena said. "When someone misuses the truth and uses one truth to kill another truth, then there is a battle between a devil and an angel. These vows you make to me belong to Hermia. Have you forgotten her? If you weigh the oaths you now make to me and the oaths you have made to her, they will weigh exactly the same. Neither scale will outweigh the other, and both scales will be full of lies."

"I lacked sound judgment when I swore to Hermia that I loved her," Lysander said.

"And I think that you lack good judgment now that you have forgotten her," Helena replied.

"Demetrius loves her, and he does not love you," Lysander said loudly.

Demetrius awoke, saw Helena, and said, "Helena, goddess, nymph, perfect, divine! To what, my love, shall I compare your eyes? Crystal is muddy compared to them. How ripe in show do your lips, those kissing cherries, tempting grow! That newly fallen white, high mountain snow, fanned by the Eastern wind, turns the color of a crow when compared to the color of your hand. Let me your hand kiss, which is that of a princess of pure white and a promise of bliss!"

Helena said, "Oh, spite! Oh, Hell! I see you all are bent to join against me for your merriment. If you were civilized and understood courtesy, you would not do to me all this injury. I know that you hate me, indeed I do, but why must you join together to mock me, too? If you were men, as men you are in show, you would not treat a gentle lady so. You vow and swear that you do love me, and you superpraise my parts, but I know that you two hate me with all your hearts. You men both are rivals, and both of you love Hermia. And you are both rivals in mocking me. This is a 'splendid' exploit, a 'manly' enterprise, done to conjure tears up in a poor maiden's eyes so at her you can laugh! No one of a noble sort would so offend a virgin, and extort the patience of a maiden, all to make you laugh."

"You are unkind, Demetrius," Lysander said. "Be not so. You love Hermia; this you know I know. And here, with all good will, with all my heart, all of Hermia's love for me I yield up to you. So give to me all of Helena's love for you — grant me my request. Helena is the woman whom I love and will love until my death."

Disgusted, Helena said, "Never did mockers waste more idle breath."

Demetrius said, "Lysander, keep your Hermia. I do not want her. If ever I was of her fond, all of that love is gone. When I gave my heart to her, my heart was like a guest travelling away from its domain. But now my heart has returned home to Helena, and there it shall remain."

"Helena, he lies," Lysander said. "Do not believe him."

"Do not disparage a love to which you cannot come near, or you will regret it," Demetrius said. "But, look, here comes your dear."

Hermia arrived on the scene, saw Lysander, and said to him, "Dark night, that from the eyes sight away takes, the ears more keen of hearing makes. Although night does impair the seeing sense, it pays the hearing sense a double recompense. Not by my eyes have I you, Lysander, found; instead, my ears brought to me your voice's sound, but why did you unkindly leave me so?"

"Why should I stay, when love did press me to go?"

"What love could take Lysander from my side?"

"Lysander's love would not let him stay by your side," Lysander said. "I love beautiful Helena, who more enlightens the night than the Moon and the stars that are the eyes of light in the night. Why did you try to find me? Didn't my leaving you let you know that I hate you?"

"You cannot be saying the truth!" Hermia said. "You cannot mean what you say!"

Helena was certain that Hermia was mocking her: "Lo, Hermia is one of this confederacy! Now I see that they have planned all three to fashion this false trick to spite me! Insulting Hermia! Most ungrateful maiden! Why have you conspired, why have you with these two men contrived to mock me with this foul derision? Is all the talk that we two have shared, the vows to be like sisters, the hours that we have spent together never wishing to be parted — have you forgotten all of that? Have you forgotten all our school days of friendship and of childhood innocence? We, Hermia, like two artists working together, have with our needles created both one flower as we both worked on one sampler, sitting on one cushion, singing one song, both in one key, as if our hands, our sides, our voices, and our minds had been those of one person. So we grew together, like a double cherry, two cherries on one stem, seeming to be parted, but yet united. Likewise, in appearance we had two bodies, but yet we had only one heart. We were like a coat of arms that represented two people. Are you willing to tear apart our long-time friendship by joining with these two men in mocking me? Doing that is not friendly, and it is not maidenly. The entire female sex, as well as me, may rebuke you for it, even though I alone do feel the injury."

"I am amazed at your passionate words," Hermia replied. "I scorn you not; it seems that you scorn me."

"Haven't you persuaded Lysander to mock me, to follow me, and to praise my eyes and face?" Helena asked. "And haven't you persuaded your other love, Demetrius, who recently threatened to kick me, to call me goddess, nymph, divine and rare, precious and celestial? Who would speak these things to a woman he hates? And why does Lysander deny his love of you, so rich within his soul, and tender me affection, unless you made him do it? I am not as much in favor as you, or as loved, or as fortunate; instead, I am miserable because I, who love, am unloved. You should pity me, not despise me."

"I don't understand what you mean by this," Hermia replied.

"Go on, continue to counterfeit serious looks, make faces at me when I turn my back, wink at each other, and keep up this joke. If you carry it out well, this joke will be talked about for years. If you have any pity, grace, or manners, you would not make me such a butt of your joke. But farewell. I am the butt of your joke partly because I followed all of you here, but my death or my absence shall soon remedy that."

"Stay, gentle Helena; hear my plea to you," Lysander said. "You are my love, my life, my soul, fair Helena!"

"Don't you ever stop?" Helena said.

Hermia said to Lysander, "Dear, do not mock her so."

Demetrius said to Lysander, "If she cannot persuade you to stop mocking Helena, I can force you to stop mocking her."

"Neither you nor she can stop me from worshipping Helena," Lysander said to Demetrius. "Your threats have no more strength than Hermia's weak requests."

Lysander then said, "Helena, I love you. I swear it by my life. I swear by that which I will lose for you, to prove him false who says that I do not love you."

Demetrius said to Helena, "I say that I love you more than he can do."

"If you say you do," Lysander said, "come and fight me and prove your words are true."

"Let's do it!" Demetrius said.

Hermia asked, "Lysander, what is going on?"

She grabbed Lysander and held on to him, preventing him from leaving to fight Demetrius.

Lysander shouted at her, "Go, away, you addict to tanning beds!"

This society preferred light skin to dark skin.

"Lysander is not serious about fighting me," Demetrius said. "He will put on an act, storm and shout, pretend to want to leave to fight me, but find an excuse the fight to back out."

He said to Lysander, "You're only half a man."

Lysander yelled at Hermia, "Let go of me, you cat, you burr! You vile thing, let loose, or I will shake you from me like a serpent!"

"Why are you grown so violent?" Hermia asked him. "Why have you changed, darling —"

"Don't 'darling' me!" Lysander raged. "Get away from me, tawny tabby! Get away from me, loathed medicine! Hated potion, get away from me!"

"You must be joking!" Hermia said to Lysander.

"He is," Helena said, "and you are also joking."

"Demetrius, I will keep my word and fight you," Lysander said.

"Would you like to bet?" Demetrius said. "Hermia has her arms around you and is preventing you from leaving with me and fighting me. It looks to me as if you aren't fighting very hard to get away from Hermia."

"Should I hurt her, strike her, kill her dead?" Lysander replied. "Although I hate her, I'll not harm a hair of her head."

"Can you do me any greater harm than to hate me?" Hermia asked Lysander. "Why should you hate me? Why? Aren't I Hermia? Aren't you Lysander? I am as pretty now as I was a while ago. When the night began, you loved me, but since the night began you left me. Why did you leave me? Did you really mean to leave me?"

"Yes, I did," Lysander said, "and I hoped to never see you again. Therefore, be out of hope, of question, of doubt; instead, be certain that nothing is truer than that it is no joke that I do hate you and I do love Helena."

Hermia turned her attention to Helena: "You trickster! You thief of love! You boyfriend-stealer! You have come to this forest this night and stolen the man I love!"

"Have you no modesty, no maidenly shame, no touch of bashfulness?" Helena asked. "Will you tear answers from my throat before I have a chance to speak? You are not a real woman! You are a counterfeit! You are a puppet!"

"A puppet!" Hermia shouted. "Now I understand what is going on. Helena has used her height to steal my boyfriend. Helena has compared her height, her tall height, to my shortness, and now my Lysander belongs to her."

She shouted at Helena, "And are you grown so high in Lysander's esteem because I am so dwarfish and so low? How low am I, you tall painted maypole? Tell me: How low am I? I may be short, but my fingernails can still reach your eyes!"

Helena was afraid: "Please, although you are mocking me, gentlemen, let her not hurt me. I was never assertive. I have no gift for standing up for myself. My reputation for cowardice is well deserved. Don't let her hit me. You perhaps may think that because she is somewhat shorter than myself, that I am a match for her, but I am not."

"Shorter!" Hermia shouted. "Do you have to keep saying that I am short?"

Helena replied, "Good Hermia, do not be so angry at me. I always did love you, Hermia. I always kept your secrets, and I have never wronged you, except that, because I love Demetrius, I told him of your flight into this forest. He followed you, and because I love him I followed him. But he has been angry at me and threatened me. He has threatened to strike me, spurn me, and even to kill me. And now, if you will let me, a fool, quietly go, I will return to Athens and follow you no further. Please, let me go. I am a simple and foolish woman."

Still angry, Hermia said, "Why, get you gone! What is stopping you?"

"A foolish heart," Helena said, "but I will leave it here."

"What, with Lysander?" Hermia shouted.

"No, with Demetrius."

"Helena, be not afraid," Lysander said, "Hermia shall not harm you."

"No, she won't," Demetrius said, "not even if Lysander here is on Hermia's side."

Still afraid, Helena said, "When she's angry, she is keen and sharp-tongued! She was sometimes a mean girl when she was in school, and though she be but little, she is fierce."

"'Little' again!" Hermia complained. "She keeps calling me 'low' and 'little.' Why do you men allow her to say such things about me? You won't do anything about it, but I will!"

Hermia let go of Lysander and started toward Helena, but Lysander and Demetrius quickly blocked her way.

Lysander said to her, "Go away, you dwarf, you minimus, you user of growth-stunting tobacco, you bead, you acorn."

"You are too ready to rise to the defense of a woman who scorns your service," Demetrius said to Lysander. "Let Helena alone. Don't talk about her. Don't try to 'help' her. If you continue to pretend to show even a little interest in her, you shall regret it."

"Hermia has let go of me and is not preventing me from leaving," Lysander said. "Follow me, if you dare, and fight me to see who gets Helena."

"Follow you!" Demetrius said. "No, I will walk beside you, cheek by jowl."

The two men departed, leaving Helena and Hermia alone.

"You are the cause of all this turmoil," Hermia said, walking toward Helena, who backed away from her. "Don't back away from me."

"I will not trust you enough to let you close to me," Helena said, "and I will no longer stay in your cursed company. Your hands are quicker than mine for a fray. My legs are longer, though, to run away."

Helena ran away.

Confused by recent events, Hermia said, "I am amazed and know not what to say."

Hermia then ran after Helena.

"All of this is your fault," Oberon said to Puck. "You keep making accidental mistakes, or perhaps, you make your mistakes accidentally on purpose."

"Believe me, King of shadows, these mistakes are accidental," Puck said. "Didn't you tell me I should know the man by the Athenian clothing he had on? And so far blameless proves my enterprise, that I have anointed an Athenian's eyes. Still, I am glad events did so pass because this their arguing I think is worth a laugh."

"Let's make things right," Oberon said. "The two male lovers are seeking a place to fight. Therefore, Robin Goodfellow, make overcast the night. Make fog dim the starry sky and lead these testy rivals so astray that one comes not within the other's way. Similar to Lysander's sometimes make your tongue, and then make Demetrius angry — for you that should be fun. Sometimes shout in the voice of Demetrius and use these lovers' voices to lead each lover away from the other. Keep them seeking each other until over their brows death-like sleep with leaden legs and bat-like wings does creep. When they are asleep, then squeeze the juice of this herbal antidote onto Lysander's eyelids. The juice will make everything all right. It has the power to take from him all error with his sight, and make him love again Hermia, thus ending his and her plight. When the lovers — male and female — next awake, all this night's derision shall seem like a dream and fruitless vision, and back to Athens shall the lovers wend, matched correctly with a love that shall never end."

He added, "While I in this affair do you employ, I will go to my Queen and ask for her boy who comes from the East, and then I will release her charmed eyes from loving a monster, and reigning again shall be peace."

"My fairy lord, this must be done with haste," Puck said. "The dragons that draw the chariot of night are nearing their home, and in the East I see the morning star, at whose approach ghosts, wandering here and far, go home to their churchyards. Other damned spirits, those of suicides who were buried at crossroads and those of people who drowned in floods and whose bodies were never recovered, already to their wormy beds have gone for fear that day should look upon them — they willfully exile themselves from light and must forever consort with black-browed night."

"But we are spirits of another sort," Oberon said, "I in the morning's light have often made sport. Far from being driven away by the coming of day, we fairy spirits are able to enjoy it and stay, although we prefer the Moonlit night to the morning light. Like the keeper of a royal forest, I often tread the groves until the full morning Sunlight, all fiery red, shines down on the ocean with fair blessed beams, and turns into yellow gold the ocean's salty green streams. Nevertheless, Puck, act quickly and make no delay. We may be able to set everything to rights before day."

Oberon flew away to go to Titania.

"Up and down, up and down, I will lead them up and down. I am feared in field and town," Puck said. "Robin Hobgoblin, lead them up and down. Here comes one."

Lysander came near and shouted, "Where are you, proud Demetrius? Speak up now!"

In Demetrius' voice, Puck shouted, "Here I am, villain. My sword is drawn and ready. Where are you?"

"I will be with you immediately."

In Demetrius' voice, Puck replied, "Follow me, then, to leveler ground so we can fight."

Lysander left, following — he thought — Demetrius' voice.

Demetrius came near and shouted, "Lysander, speak again! You runaway, you coward, have you fled? Speak! Are you cowering in some bush? Where are you hiding your head?"

Puck shouted in Lysander's voice, "You coward, you are bragging to the stars and telling the bushes that you are looking for me near and far, yet you will not come and fight me. Come, coward! Come, child! I'll whip you with a rod. Anyone who draws a sword on you is defiled."

Demetrius shouted, "Where are you?"

Puck shouted in Lysander's voice, "Follow my voice. This is not a good place to fight."

They left, but soon Lysander returned, stumbled in the darkness, and complained, "He goes before me and continuously dares me to come on, but when I come to where he called, then he is gone. The villain is much lighter-heeled than me. I followed fast, but faster he did flee. I am fallen into a dark uneven way, and here will I rest myself and stay."

He lay down and said, "Come, gentle day! Once you show me your light, I will find Demetrius and get revenge for this spite."

He slept.

Soon, Puck led Demetrius near Lysander.

Puck shouted in Lysander's voice, "Coward, why are you avoiding me?"

"Wait for me, if you dare," Demetrius shouted. "I know well that you are running away from me. You keep changing your position, and you dare not stay in one place and look me in the face. Where are you now?"

"Come here," Puck shouted in Lysander's voice. "Here I am."

"Not for long," Demetrius said. "You will be gone by the time I get there and so you do me wrong. You shall dearly pay for mocking me this night if ever I see your face in daylight. Now, go your way. I am tired, and on this cold ground I will make my bed. When morning arrives, expect me to break your head."

He lay on the ground and slept.

Helena arrived and complained, "Oh, weary night! Oh, long and tedious night, make your hours shorter! May dawn soon shine in the East so that I may go back to Athens by daylight and escape my former friends who now detest me. Sleep, who for a time stops sorrow, keep me from my misery."

Helena lay on the ground and slept.

Puck said, "Yet but three? I need one more — two of both kinds make up four. Here she comes, cursed and sad. Cupid is a knavish lad, thus to make poor females mad."

Hermia arrived and complained, "I have been never so weary, never so in woe. Bedabbled with the dew and torn with briers, I can no further crawl, no further go. My legs cannot keep pace with my desires. Here will I rest until the break of light. May Heaven protect Lysander if there is a fight!"

Hermia lay on the ground and slept.

Puck said to all four lovers, "On the ground, sleep sound."

To Lysander, he said, "I'll apply to your eyes, gentle lover, something that will make you truly love the one you should love when her you spy."

Puck squeezed the juice of the herbal antidote onto Lysander's sleeping eyelids, and then he said, "When you wake, you will take true delight in the sight of your former lady's eyes. And the country proverb by all men known, that every man should have his own, in your waking shall be shown. Jack shall have Jill; nothing shall go ill, and each man and woman shall be matched well."

CHAPTER 4

— 4.1 —

In another part of the forest, Titania entertained Bottom. Many other fairies, including Peaseblossom, Cobweb, Mote, and Mustardseed, were also present. Oberon watched from a position where he was unseen.

Titania said to Bottom, who was enjoying himself, "Come, sit down upon this flowery bed, while I your lovely cheeks caress, and stick musk-roses in the hair of your sleek, smooth head, and kiss your beautiful, large ears, my gentle joy and boy-toy."

Bottom asked, "Where's Peaseblossom?"

"Here I am."

"Scratch my head, please, Peaseblossom. Where's Monsieur Cobweb?"

"Here I am."

"Monsieur Cobweb, good monsieur, please get you your weapons in your hand, and kill me a red-hipped bumblebee on the top of a thistle; and, good monsieur, bring me the honeybag. Do not tire yourself too much doing this, monsieur; and, good monsieur, be careful not to break the honeybag; I would hate for you to be covered with honey. Where's Monsieur Mustardseed?"

"Here I am," he said, bowing repeatedly.

"Shake hands with me, Monsieur Mustardseed, and please stop bowing, good monsieur."

"What can I do for you?"

"Nothing, good monsieur, but to help Cavalier Cobweb to scratch my head. I must go to the barber soon, monsieur; for I think that I am marvelously hairy about the face; and I am such a tender ass, if my hair do but tickle me, I must scratch."

"Would you like to hear some music, my sweet love?" Titania asked Bottom.

"I have a reasonably good ear in music," Bottom replied. "Let's have something with lots of clacking and clapping."

"Or would you prefer something sweet to eat?"

"I could peck at a pound of provender. I could munch a bunch of good dry oats. I have a great desire to eat a bundle of hay — good hay, sweet hay, has no equal."

"I will have a venturesome fairy seek a squirrel's hoard, and he will fetch you new nuts."

"I prefer to eat a handful or two of dried peas," Bottom said, "but, please, let none of your people disturb me, for now an exposition for sleep has come upon me."

"You mean a disposition for sleep, dear," Titania said. "You sleep, and I will hold you in my arms. Fairies, go now, and stay away for a while."

The fairies departed, and Titania said to Bottom, who was now asleep. "I will hold you in my arms the way that sweet honeysuckle gently twists itself around the strong trunk of an elm. How I love you!"

Titania fell asleep beside the sleeping Bottom.

Puck arrived, and Oberon said, "Welcome, Robin Goodfellow. Do you see this sweet sight? I begin to pity her lovesickness now. I recently met with her as she was seeking treats for this silly fool, and I scolded her because of the silly way she was acting. She had placed on this ass' head a coronet of fresh and fragrant flowers. Drops of dew, which sometimes appear on buds and swell like round and lustrous pearls, were on the coronet, standing in the pretty flowerets' eyes like tears that did their own disgrace bewail. After I had scolded her, Titania with mild words spoke to me. I then did ask her to give me the changeling child, and immediately she gave him to me and sent a fairy to bear him to my bower in Fairyland."

Oberon added, "Now that I have the boy, I will undo this hateful imperfection of Titania's eyes. And, gentle Puck, take this ass' head off this Athenian fool, so that, when he awakens when the other Athenians do, they may all go back to Athens and think that this night's incidents are only a disconcerting dream. But first I will release the fairy Queen."

He squeezed the juice of the herbal antidote onto Titania's sleeping eyelids and said, "Be as you used to be; see as you used to see. Blessed be Diana, the Moon-goddess. Diana's herb over Cupid's flower has such force and blessed power. Now, my Titania, wake up, my sweet Queen."

Titania, who thought that she had been dreaming, was happy to see Oberon, her husband: "My Oberon! What visions have I seen! I dreamed that I loved an ass!"

Oberon gestured toward the sleeping Bottom and said, "There lies your love."

Titania looked down and beside her, saw Bottom, and was shocked: "How came this thing to pass? Oh, how I hate now to look at this ass!"

Like many, many mortal women in similar positions, Titania thought, *What was I thinking!*

Oberon said to Titania, "We will talk about this later."

To Puck, he said, "Robin, take off this ass' head."

To Titania, he said, "Call for magical music that will make these five sleeping mortals sleep the deepest sleep."

Titania ordered, "Music! Music that will charm mortals and make them sleep so deep!"

Music began to play.

Puck removed the ass' head from Bottom and said to him, "When you wake up, you will not see with this ass' eyes — you will see with your own ass' eyes."

Oberon said, "Come, my Queen, hold hands with me, and we will dance on the ground where these sleepers be."

They danced and then Oberon said to Titania, "Now you and I newly enjoy amity, and we will tomorrow at midnight ceremoniously dance in Duke Theseus' house joyfully. We shall bless his house with prosperity and there shall these four lovers wedded be, along with Theseus and Hippolyta, happily."

Puck said, "Fairy King, hark — I do hear the morning lark."

Oberon said to Titania, "My Queen, you who sit quietly thinking, we can run toward and rejoin the night soon. We can fly around the globe quickly, swifter than the wandering Moon."

Titania replied, "During our flight, tell me how it came this night that I sleeping here was found with these mortals on the ground."

The fairies flew away.

Hunting horns sounded in the distance. Theseus was taking Hippolyta hunting, a good entertainment for an Amazon. Egeus and others also participated in the hunt.

Theseus said, "Go, one of you, find the forester. We have finished our ceremony of the rites of May, and since we are still in the morning of this day, Hippolyta, whom I love, shall hear the music of my hounds. Tell him to unleash the hounds in the western valley and let them bound."

An attendant left to find the forester.

Theseus said to Hippolyta, "We will, fair Queen, go up to the mountain's top, and listen to the music of my hounds and the mountain's echoes."

Hippolyta enjoyed this kind of entertainment: "I was with Hercules and Cadmus once, when in a forest of Crete their hounds of Sparta brought to bay a bear. Never did I hear such gallant music — the groves, the skies, the waterfalls, and the echoes of every region nearby seemed to be all filled with one mutual cry. I never heard so musical a sound — it was such sweet thunder."

Theseus said, "My hounds have been bred from Spartan dams and sires. They have the Spartan hounds' hanging cheeks and sandy color. From their heads hang ears that sweep away the morning dew. They are crooked-kneed and dew-lapped like Thessalian bulls. Slow in pursuit they may be, but they are matched in mouth like bells of harmonious tones to create a tuneful melody of the hunt. The hunting pack creates a cry more melodious and beautiful than any ever created with human voice or with hunting horn — not even in Crete, in Sparta, or in Thessaly. You may judge for yourself when you hear their cries."

Theseus caught sight of some bodies lying together on the edge of the forest and asked, "What nymphs are these?"

Egeus rode over to Theseus and said, "My lord, this is my daughter here asleep, and this man is Lysander. This man is

Demetrius, and here is Helena, the daughter of old Nedar. I wonder how they came to be here together.”

“No doubt they rose up early to observe the rite of May,” Theseus said. “Knowing that we would be hunting here, they came here to watch. But, Egeus, isn’t this the day that Hermia should tell us whether or not she will marry Demetrius?”

“Yes, it is, my lord.”

Theseus ordered an attendant, “Go and tell the huntsmen to wake them with their horns.”

The attendant left to tell the huntsmen, and soon the huntsmen blew their horns loudly. Lysander, Demetrius, Helena, and Hermia all woke up.

Theseus joked, “Good morning, friends. Lovebirds are said to begin to mate on Saint Valentine’s Day, but Saint Valentine’s Day has passed. Do you lovebirds begin to couple only now?”

“I beg your pardon, my lord,” Lysander said.

“Please, young lovers, stand up,” Theseus said. “Lysander and Demetrius, I know that you are — or have been — enemies. How did your gentle concord — and concord it must be because you sleep by each other so peacefully —come into the world? How can two enemies sleep side by side with no fear of harm?”

“My lord, I shall reply perplexedly, half asleep and half awake,” Lysander replied. “I swear that I cannot truly say how I came here, but as I think — and truly would I speak — I believe that I came with Hermia so we could flee from out of the range of the harsh Athenian law.”

Egeus said, “Enough, enough. My lord, you have heard enough. I beg the law, the law, upon his head. Lysander and my daughter would have stolen away; they would, Demetrius, thereby have stolen from you and me. They would have stolen away your future wife and my right to choose the man whom my daughter will marry."

Demetrius spoke up: "My lord, beautiful Helena told me of their plan and of their purpose in coming to this forest. Out of fury, I followed them, and out of love, Helena followed me. But, my good lord, I don't know by what power — but by some power it has happened — my love for Hermia has melted like the snow. My love for Hermia seems to me now like the memory of a worthless trinket that I loved when I was a child. Now, I love only Helena. Only she is the object and the pleasure of my eye. All the faith and all the virtue of my heart are for Helena alone. I was engaged to marry her, my lord, before I ever saw Hermia. But somehow, as if I were ill, this food I had loved I came to hate. But now I am like a person restored to health and his natural taste, and I long for that food. Now I do wish for Helena, love Helena, long for Helena, and will for evermore be true to Helena."

"Lovers, this is a fortunate meeting," Theseus said. "We will hear more about your experiences later."

To Egeus, Theseus said, "Earlier, I said that I can by no means extenuate the law of Athens, but I do exactly that now. Egeus, I do overrule your will. Your daughter shall marry Lysander, and Helena shall marry Demetrius. In the temple later this day, these couples shall eternally be knit, as shall be Hippolyta and me."

Pleased at Theseus' ruling, Hippolyta smiled.

Theseus said, "Now that the morning is nearly over, let's stop our hunt. Let all of us, including the couples who will be married later, return to Athens. There, we will enjoy a festive feast."

He turned to his betrothed and said, "Come, Hippolyta."

Theseus, Hippolyta, Egeus, and others departed, leaving behind Lysander and Hermia, and Demetrius and Helena.

"What happened last night?" Demetrius asked. "The events of last night seem far away and murky, like a distant mountain whose top is hidden by clouds."

"I remember the events of last night as if I were seeing them with eyes unfocused and seeing double," Hermia said.

"I remember the events the same way," Helena said. "I have found Demetrius, but I have found him like I could find a jewel. The jewel is in my possession for now, but someone could come along and claim it as hers."

"Are you sure that we are awake?" Demetrius asked. "It seems to me that yet we sleep and dream. Was the Duke really here, and did he tell us to follow him?"

"Yes," Hermia said, "and my father was also here."

"And Hippolyta," Helena said.

"And the Duke really did tell us to follow him to the temple," Lysander said.

"Why, then, we are awake," Demetrius said. "Let's follow the Duke, and as we walk let us tell each other our dreams."

The four young lovers walked away, and Bottom, who had been sleeping at some distance from the lovers, woke up, saying, "When my cue comes, call me, and I will answer. My next cue is 'Most fair Pyramus.'"

Bottom looked around, saw no one, and called, "Peter Quince! Flute, the bellows-mender! Snout, the tinker!

Starveling! Snug! My word, they have gone home and left me here asleep!"

He paused, thought, and said, "I have had a most rare vision. I have had a dream, past the wit of man to say what dream it was — man is but an ass, if he would try to explain this dream. I thought I was — no man can tell what. I thought I was, and I thought I had — but a man would have to be a motley-wearing fool if he would try to say what I thought I had."

Bottom felt the top of his head above both ears, and then he said, "The eye of man has not heard, the ear of man has not seen, man's hand is not able to taste, his tongue able to conceive, nor his heart able to report, what my dream was."

Bottom thought, and then he said, "I will get Peter Quince to write a ballet of this dream. It shall be called 'Bottom's Dream,' because it has no bottom; and I will sing it in the latter end of our play, before the Duke. Perhaps, to show the ballet to better advantage, I shall sing it when Thisby dies."

— 4.2 —

Quince, Flute, Snout, and Starveling were meeting in Peter Quince's house in Athens.

Quince asked Starveling, "Have you sent anyone to Bottom's house to ask about him? Has he come home yet?"

"No one has seen him," Starveling replied. "No doubt, the fairies have carried him away."

"If he cannot be found, then the play is ruined, isn't it?" Flute said. "We cannot perform it, can we?"

"That would be impossible," Quince replied. "In all of Athens, no one but Bottom can play the part of Pyramus."

"That's true," Flute said. "Bottom has simply the best wit of all the craftsmen in Athens."

"Yes, and he is the most handsome, too," Quince said. "And he is a very paramour for a sweet voice."

"You must say 'paragon,'" Flute said. "A paramour is, God bless us, a wicked thing."

Snug knocked on Quince's door and entered the house and said, "Friends, the Duke is coming from the temple. He and Hippolyta have been married, and so have two other couples. If we had been able to put on our play, we would all have been made men — we would have received a pension for life."

"Sweet friend Bottom!" Flute said. "I wish you were here! You would be able to earn for yourself a pension of sixpence a day for the rest of your life. I'll be hanged if you would not have earned a pension of sixpence a day for playing Pyramus. Bottom would have deserved it, too. For playing Pyramus, he would have gotten sixpence a day — or nothing."

Bottom now knocked on Quince's door and entered the house, saying, "Where are these lads! Where are these good fellows! Hello, friends!"

"Bottom!" Quince said happily. "Oh, most courageous day! Oh, most happy hour!"

"Friends, I have wonders to recount," Bottom said, "but do not ask me about them, for if I tell you, I am no true Athenian."

He paused and then said, "I will tell you everything, exactly as it happened."

"Let us hear, sweet Bottom," Quince requested.

"I won't say a word," Bottom said, "but I will tell you that the Duke has dined. Get your costumes together. Get good strings to use to attach your false beards, and new ribbons to use to tie your shoes. Let us go to the palace right away. Every actor, look over your part. The long and the short of it is that our play is on a list of the entertainments that Theseus shall choose from to see. Let Thisby have clean linen, and let not him who plays the lion pare his fingernails, for they shall hang out for the lion's claws. And, most dear actors, eat no onions or garlic, for we are to utter sweet breath, and I have no doubt but that we shall hear the audience say, 'It is a sweet comedy.' Most important of all, adjust your testicles. No actor can perform competently unless the two stones in his pants are sitting comfortably. No more words, friends! Let's go!"

CHAPTER 5

In the palace, Theseus and Hippolyta were talking. Philostrate and others were also present.

Hippolyta said, "Theseus, these four lovers have talked of strange things."

"I think that they have talked of things that are more strange than they are true," Theseus replied. "I never believe old fables or fairy tales. Lovers and madmen have such frenzied brains, such fertile imaginations, that they see — or imagine that they see — much more than cool reason ever comprehends. The lunatic, the lover, and the poet are all made by imagination. The lunatic sees more devils than vast Hell can hold. The lover, just as frantic as the lunatic, sees the beauty of Helen of Troy in the dark face of an exotic dancer. The poet's eye, in a fine frenzy rolling, glances from Heaven to Earth, and from Earth to Heaven. As imagination gives birth to things unknown, the poet's pen writes them down as if they were real and gives to airy nothing a local habitation and a name. A strong imagination tricks us. If a strong imagination senses some joy, it creates some bringer — perhaps a god — of that joy. At night, when someone senses some fear, how easy is a bush imagined to be a bear!"

"But the four lovers all told the same story of the night," Hippolyta said. "Their stories agreed with each other, and that consistency to me is evidence that whatever happened — no matter how strange and to be wondered at — is more than imaginary fantasies."

Lysander, Hermia, Demetrius, and Helena all walked into the great chamber.

Theseus said to Hippolyta, "Here come the lovers, full of joy and mirth."

To the four lovers, he said, "Joy, gentle friends! May joy and the fresh days of love always accompany your hearts!"

"May more joy and more love always be found in your royal estates, at your table, and in your bed," Lysander replied.

"Now, what entertainments — perhaps dancers, masked or unmasked — shall we enjoy?" Theseus said. "We have a long age of three hours to pass between now and our bedtime. Where is our usual manager of mirth? What revels are at hand? Is there no play to ease the anguish of a torturing hour? Call Philostrate."

"Here I am, mighty Theseus," Philostrate said.

"What entertainments to pass the time have you for this evening?" Theseus asked. "What masked dance? What music? How shall we quickly pass this slow-moving time, if not with some delightful entertainment?"

Philostrate handed Theseus a piece of paper and said, "Here is a list of the entertainments offered. Please choose which your highness will see first."

Theseus read out loud, "'*The battle with the Centaurs, to be sung by an Athenian eunuch accompanied by the harp.*' We will have none of that, for the obvious reason. Beside, I have told my lovely Hippolyta that story in honor of my kinsman Hercules.

"'*The riot of the tipsy Bacchanals, tearing the Thracian singer in their rage.*' No, this will not do. This is an old entertainment.

It was played when I from Thebes came most recently a conqueror.

"'*The thrice three Muses mourning for the death of Learning, late deceased in beggary.*' We will have none of that because it is some satire, keen and critical, hardly the thing to hear after a wedding ceremony.

"'*A tedious brief scene of young Pyramus and his love Thisby; very tragical mirth.*' Merry and tragical! Tedious and brief! You may as well talk about hot ice and similarly strange snow."

Theseus asked Philostrate, "How shall we find the concord of this discord?"

Philostrate said, "A play there is, my lord, some ten words long, which is as brief as I have known a play; but by ten words, my lord, it is too long, which makes it tedious; for in all the play there is not one word apt or one player well cast. And tragical, my noble lord, it is, because Pyramus in the play does kill himself, which, when I saw rehearsed, I must confess, made my eyes cry; but more merry tears the passion of loud laughter never shed."

"Who are they who do play it?" Theseus asked.

"Men with calloused hands who work here in Athens," Philostrate said. "They have never labored in their minds until now. They have taxed their unexercised brains to create this play to celebrate your wedding."

"And we will hear it," Theseus said.

"No, my noble lord," Philostrate said. "It is not for you. I have seen the play, and it is nothing, nothing in the world. There is nothing in it to bring you pleasure, except perhaps that you may take pleasure in their good intentions and in how hard they have worked — and it has been hard work for them —

to make this play and to learn their lines. All of this they have done to do you service."

"I will hear that play," Theseus said. "Nothing can be amiss when it is presented with sincerity and a sense of duty. Go, bring them in."

Philostrate left, and Theseus said, "Please sit down, ladies."

All sat down, but Hippolyta said, "Should we see this play? I don't want to see working-class people attempt to do something that they are incapable of doing and embarrassing themselves when they are trying their best to serve you."

"Why, gentle, sweet Hippolyta, you shall see no such thing," Theseus said.

"But Philostrate says that they can do nothing right in this play."

"Then the kinder we will be, to give them thanks for nothing," Theseus said. "Our entertainment shall be to take as correctly done that in which they make mistakes. Whatever they cannot correctly do, we can generously judge their performance in accordance with their good intentions, not in accordance with their bad performance. In places where I have come, people have intended to greet me with premeditated welcomes. But I have seen them shiver and look pale, make periods in the midst of sentences, and throttle their practiced speeches because of their stage fright. I have seen them completely break down and be able to say nothing. Objectively, they have not paid me a welcome. Trust me, sweet, out of this silence I have subjectively found a welcome. In their stage fright and modest and dutiful attempt to do what they could not but wished that they could, I have found as much welcome as I would from the rattling tongue of confident and bold eloquence. Love and tongue-tied innocence say much, I believe, although not in words."

Philostrate returned and said, "So please your grace, the Prologue is ready."

"Let him approach," Theseus said.

Trumpets sounded, and Quince came on stage to say the prologue:

"If we offend, it is with our good will.

"That you should think, we come not to offend

"but with good will. To show our simple skill,

"that is the true beginning of our end.

"Consider then we come but in despite.

"We do not come as intending to content you,

"our true intent is. All for your delight

"we are not here. That you should here repent you,

"the actors are at hand and by their show

"you shall know all that you are likely to know."

Theseus had said to Hippolyta that often people who intended to greet him would make periods in the midst of their sentences. Such was the case here. Quince had badly recited his prologue, and it had come out in a way that was insulting to the audience.

This is what Quince had meant to say:

"If we offend, it is with our good will

"that you should think we come, not to offend,

"but with good will to show our simple skill:

"That is the true beginning of our end.

"Consider then we come — but in despite

"we do not come — as intending to content you.

"Our true intent is all for your delight:

"We are not here that you should here repent you.

"The actors are at hand and by their show

"you shall know all that you are likely to know."

Amused, Theseus laughed and said, "This speaker does not understand how to use periods at the ends of sentences."

As he had said to Hippolyta, Theseus was able to find a subjective welcome where no objective welcome existed. If he were a different kind of ruler, he could have had Quince executed.

The other noble members of the audience followed Theseus' lead: They were amused and not angry when they talked about Quince.

Lysander said, "He has ridden his prologue like a colt that is being broken. The colt does not know how to stop, and this speaker does not know to stop briefly at the ends of sentences. One can learn from this, my lord. It is not enough just to speak — one must also speak correctly."

Even Hippolyta was amused: "Indeed he has played on his prologue like a child plays a flute that he is attempting to learn. The flute makes sounds, but it does not make music."

"His speech was like a tangled chain," Theseus said. "No link or word was broken, but the chain of links or words is all disordered."

Theseus laughed and said, "Who is up next?"

While the royal members of the audience had been talking, Pyramus and Thisby, Wall, Moonshine, and Lion had come onstage. While Quince recited the next part of his prologue, the actors pantomimed their parts.

Quince recited, "Gentlepeople, perhaps you wonder at this show;

"but wonder on, until truth makes all things plain.
"This man is Pyramus, if you would like to know;
"this beauteous lady Thisby is not plain.
"This man, with limestone and cement, doth present
"Wall, that vile Wall which did these lovers sunder;
"and through Wall's chink, poor souls, they are content
"to whisper. At this let no man wonder.
"This man, with lantern, dog, and bushel of thorn,
"presenteth Moonshine; for, if you will know,
"by Moonshine did these lovers think no scorn
"to meet at Ninus' tomb, where their love would grow.
"This grisly beast, whom Lion we do call,
"did scare away, or rather did affright;
"the trusty Thisby, coming first by night,
"and, as she fled, her mantle she let fall,
"which Lion vile with bloody mouth did stain.
"Then comes Pyramus, a sweet youth and tall,
"and finds his trusty Thisby's mantle slain:
"Whereat, with blade, with bloody blameful blade,
"he bravely broached his boiling bloody breast;
"and Thisby, tarrying in mulberry shade,
"his dagger drew, and died. For all the rest,
"let Lion, Moonshine, Wall, and lovers twain
"at large discourse, while here they do remain."

Theseus was amused by the bad poetry, and by Quince's belief that the audience needed to be told the well-known plot of the play in advance.

In a good mood brought about by a wedding that was making him happy and by a bad play that was making him laugh, Theseus said, "I wonder if the lion will speak."

Demetrius joked, "It will be no surprise if it does, my lord. One lion may speak, when many asses do."

Once Quince, Thisby, Lion, and Moonshine had exited the stage, Wall said, "In this same interlude it doth befall

"that I, one Snout by name, present a Wall;

"and such a Wall, as I would have you all think,

"that had in it a crannied hole or chink,

"through which the lovers, Pyramus and Thisby,

"did whisper often very secretly.

"This clay, this cement, and this stone do show

"that I am that same Wall; the truth is so:

"and this the cranny is, right and sinister,

"through which the fearful lovers are to whisper."

Theseus joked, "Would you desire cement, plaster, and stone to speak better?"

Demetrius replied, "It is the wittiest partition that ever I heard speak, my lord."

Bottom, playing Pyramus, strode onstage.

"Pyramus draws near the wall," Theseus said. "Silence!"

Pyramus recited, "Oh, grim-looked night! Oh, night with hue so black!

"Oh, night, which ever art when day is not!

"Oh, night! Oh, night! Alack, alack, alack,

"I fear my Thisby's promise is forgot!

"And thou, oh, Wall! Oh, sweet, oh, lovely Wall,

"That stands between her father's ground and mine!

"Thou, Wall! Oh, Wall! Oh, sweet and lovely Wall,

"show me thy chink, to blink through with my eyne!"

Wall held up his fingers in an OK sign.

Pyramus continued, "Thanks, courteous Wall! Jove shield thee well for this!

"But what see I? No Thisby do I see.

"Oh, wicked Wall, through whom I see no bliss!

"Cursed be thy stones for thus deceiving me!"

Theseus joked, "The Wall, I think, since it can talk, should curse Pyramus."

Theseus had spoken too loudly.

Bottom overheard Theseus, and breaking character as well as taking an enormous liberty, he said to him, "No, in truth, sir, he should not. 'Deceiving me' is Thisby's cue: She is to enter now, and I am to spy her through the Wall. You shall see; it will happen exactly as I have told you."

Theseus nodded and then laughed at Bottom's thinking that he needed to be told the story of Pyramus and Thisby. He also ignored the great liberty that a craftsman had taken in speaking to him, the ruler of Athens, without being spoken to first.

Bottom then said as Thisby walked onstage, "Yonder she comes."

Flute, who was playing Thisby, had remembered Bottom's earlier advice and had adjusted his two stones before coming onstage.

Thisby recited, "Oh, Wall, very often hast you heard my moans,

"for parting my fair Pyramus and me!

"My cherry lips have often kissed your stones,

"your stones with cement and hair knit up in thee."

The males in the audience especially laughed at Thisby's lines.

Helena understood the meaning of what was said a little later than the others, and she thought in shock, *Oh!*

Pyramus said, "I see a voice: now will I to the chink,

"to spy if I can hear my Thisby's face. Thisby!"

Thisby replied, "My love thou art, my love, I think."

Pyramus replied, "Think what thou wilt, I am thy lover's grace;

"and, like Limander, am I trusty still."

Theseus thought, *The mistakes multiply. 'Thy lover's grace' means 'thy gracious lover.' Also, Pyramus means Leander, the lover of the woman named Hero, a priestess of Venus. Leander swam across the Hellespont each night to visit her. She lit a lamp each night to guide his way across the narrow sea. One night, the winds blew out Hero's light, and Leander drowned. When Hero saw her lover's dead body, she committed suicide.*

Thisby replied, "And I am faithful like Helen, until the Fates me kill."

Theseus thought, *Thisby means 'Hero,' I hope. Helen of Troy will run away with Paris — she will be unfaithful to her husband, Menelaus. Of course, the Trojan War has not yet occurred, but I and many others in Athens have studied prophecies.*

Pyramus recited, "Not Shafalus to Procrus was so true."

Theseus thought, *He means Cephalus and Procris, two ancient lovers whose love ended tragically.*

Thisby replied, "As Shafalus to Procrus, I to you."

Theseus thought, *Cephalus ended up killing Procris, albeit accidentally. It's also odd that Thisby would say this sentence because Cephalus was the man and Procris was the woman.*

Pyramus said, "Oh, kiss me through the hole of this vile Wall!"

They kissed — or attempted to.

Thisby said, "I kiss the Wall's hole, not your lips at all."

The males in the audience who had laughed at Thisby's kissing the Wall's stones laughed again.

Pyramus said, "Wilt thou at Ninny's tomb meet me straightway?"

Thisby replied, "Come life, or come death, I come without delay."

Pyramus and Thisby exited.

Wall said, "Thus have I, Wall, my part discharged so;

"and, being done, thus Wall away doth go."

Wall exited.

"The lovers should have waited," Theseus said. "The Wall that separated them is now down."

"Waiting would not have helped," Demetrius said. "The Wall would have stayed around to eavesdrop."

"This is the silliest stuff that ever I heard," Hippolyta said.

"Even the best plays and actors are but shadows," Theseus said, "and the worst plays and actors are no worse than shadows, if we use our imaginations to improve them."

"It must be your imagination that does the improving," Hippolyta said. "The imaginations of this playwright and these actors have done little to make a good play."

"If we imagine no worse of them than they of themselves, they may pass for excellent men," Theseus said.

Meanwhile, Moonshine and Lion had come onstage. Moonshine carried a lantern and a bushel of thorns, and he led a dog by a leash.

Theseus said, "Here come two noble beasts in: a man and a lion."

Lion recited, "You, ladies, you, whose gentle hearts do fear
"the smallest monstrous mouse that creeps on floor,
"may now perchance both quake and tremble here,
"when Lion rough in wildest rage doth roar.
"Then know that I, one Snug the joiner, am
"a Lion fierce, and not any Lion's Mam;
"for, if I should as Lion come in strife
"into this place, at risk would be my life."

Theseus said, "I think the actor playing the Lion has mixed up his words. I think he meant to tell us that he is not a lion; instead, he has told us that he is not the mother of a lion. Still, this Lion is a very polite beast, and he acts morally and with a good conscience."

"This is the most moral Lion that I have ever seen, my lord," Demetrius said.

"This Lion is a very fox when it comes to courage," Lysander said. "He is more sly than he is brave."

"Yes, he is," Theseus said, "and he is as discreet as a goose. He is more foolish than he is discreet."

"I disagree, my lord," Demetrius said. "His courage cannot carry away his discretion, and we all know that the fox carries away the goose."

"I am sure that his discretion cannot carry away his courage," Theseus said, "because we all know that the goose does not carry away the fox. But so be it. Let us leave the Lion to his discretion, and let us listen to the Moon."

Moonshine, who had waited patiently for the nobles to stop talking, started to speak, "This lantern doth the horned Moon present —"

But the nobles were in a mood for making jokes, and they interrupted Moonshine. People who laugh often want to create more laughter.

"He should have worn the horns on his head," Demetrius said. "Cuckolds have horns."

People joked that a cuckold — a man with an unfaithful wife — had invisible horns on his head.

"A horned Moon has crescents," Theseus said, "but this Moon has no visible crescents. Therefore, his horns must be invisible inside the circle that is the Moon."

Moonshine again attempted to say his lines:

"This lantern doth the horned Moon present;

"Myself the Man in the Moon do seem to be."

Theseus interrupted again, "This is the greatest error of all — the man should be inside the lantern. How else could he be the Man in the Moon?"

"He dares not go in the lantern because of the candle," Demetrius said. "The candle is ready to be snuffed out, and he does not want to be snuffed out with it."

Hippolyta joked, "I am weary of this Moon — I wish he would change!"

"The Moon appears to have but little light and so is waning," Theseus said, "but we should be courteous and reasonable, and wait and see."

Moonshine waited patiently.

"Proceed, Moon," Lysander said.

Moonshine abandoned his poetic lines and said in prose, "All that I have to say is to tell you that the lantern is the Moon, I am the Man in the Moon, this thorn bush is my thorn bush, and this dog is my dog."

"Why, all these should be in the lantern; for all these are in the Moon," Demetrius said. "But silence! Here comes Thisby."

Thisby came on onstage and said, "This is old Ninny's tomb. Where is my love?"

The Lion roared, and Thisby screamed and ran offstage, dropping her mantle as she exited.

The Lion then got stage fright and froze. Neither the Lion nor Moonshine did or said anything.

Theseus thought, *This is the other thing that I told Hippolyta that people do when they speak to me. Some put periods in the middle of sentences, as happened during the Prologue of this play. Other people get stage fright and freeze, as is happening now.*

Theseus remembered that he ought to be courteous, as he had promised Hippolyta that he would be. The nobles felt bad that their humorous comments were having this effect on the actors. Knowing that one good reason for the Lion to get stage fright was the humorous comments that they had made to the Man in the Moon, which the Lion had heard while waiting for his cue, Theseus wanted to put the Lion at ease and to make some amends to Moonshine and the other actors.

Theseus whispered to the other nobles, "Our jokes have given the Lion stage fright. Let's say some things to encourage these actors."

"Well roared, Lion," Demetrius said loudly.

"Well run, Thisby," Theseus said.

"Well shone, Moon," Hippolyta said. "Truly, the Moon shines with a good grace."

Heartened by the praise, the Lion, recovering from stage fright, picked up Thisby's mantle in his mouth and shook it as if it were a mouse that a cat had caught.

"Well moused, Lion," Theseus said as the Lion exited.

The nobles applauded.

Lysander whispered, "And so the Lion vanished."

"And then came Pyramus," Demetrius whispered.

Bottom came onstage as Pyramus and recited, "Sweet Moon, I thank thee for thy Sunny beams;

"I thank thee, Moon, for shining now so bright;

"for, by thy gracious, golden, glittering gleams,

"I trust to take of truest Thisby sight.

"But stay! Oh, spite!

"But mark, poor knight,

"what dreadful dole is here!

"Eyes, do you see?

"How can it be?

"Oh, dainty duck! Oh, dear!

"Thy mantle good,

"What, stained with blud!"

Bottom thought, *Good, I remembered to say "blud." "Good" and "blood" are supposed to rhyme, but they can't rhyme unless their ends sound alike.*

Bottom continued, "Approach, ye Furies fell!

"Oh, Fates, come, come,

"Cut thread and thrum;

"Quail, crush, conclude, and quell!"

Theseus whispered, "Pyramus' passion — and the death of a dear friend — would go a long way in making a man feel sad."

Hippolyta joked, "Curse my heart, but I pity the man."

Pyramus recited, "Oh, why, Nature, didst thou lions frame?

"Since lion vile hath here deflowered my dear —"

Backstage, Quince thought, *Devoured — not deflowered.*

Bottom continued, "— who is — no, no — who was the fairest dame

"who lived, who loved, who liked, who looked with cheer.

"Come, tears, confound;

"out, sword, and wound"

(Bottom made sure that "confound" and "wound" rhymed.)

"the pap of Pyramus —

"aye, that left pap,

"where heart doth hop."

Pyramus stabbed himself, then said, "Thus die I, thus, thus, thus.

"Now am I dead,

"now am I fled;

"my soul is in the sky.

"Tongue, lose thy light;

"Moon, take thy flight."

No, no, no, Quince thought. *Bottom should have said, "Tongue, take thy flight / Moon, lose thy light." "Tongue, take thy flight" means to be made silent by death.*

Moonshine exited.

Pyramus waited until Moonshine's exit was complete, and then he continued, "Now die, die, die, die, die."

He died.

Demetrius whispered, "If Pyramus were throwing a die, he would throw an ace or a snake eye — one dot on top — because now he is alone."

"He would have to throw less than an ace," Lysander whispered, "because he is dead — he is nothing."

"With the help of a surgeon, he might yet recover, and show himself to be an ass again," Theseus whispered.

Hippolyta whispered, "Now that Moonshine is gone, how will Thisby see her lover when she comes back?"

Thisby had come onstage and was skipping around, not seeing Pyramus.

"She will find him by starlight," Theseus whispered back, and then he added, "Here she comes, and her passion ends the play."

Hippolyta whispered, "I think that Thisby's passionate speech and death should not last long — not for this Pyramus, anyway."

She also thought, *I already know that Thisby's passion will end the play. To show off his knowledge, Theseus insists on telling me things I already know. How like a man!*

"It's difficult to tell whether Pyramus or Thisby is the better actor," Demetrius whispered. "Either way — Pyramus as an actor in male roles, or Thisby as an actor in female roles — God help us!"

"Look," Lysander whispered, "Thisby has used her sweet eyes to see Pyramus."

"And now we will hear Thisby start moaning," Lysander whispered.

Thisby recited, "Asleep, my love?

"What, dead, my dove?

"Oh, Pyramus, arise!

"Speak, speak. Quite dumb?

"Dead, dead? A tomb

"must cover thy sweet eyes.

"These my lips,

"this cherry nose,
"these yellow cowslip cheeks,
"are gone, are gone!
"Lovers, make moan.
"His eyes were green as leeks.
"Oh, Sisters Three,
"goddesses of fate, you be,
"come, come to me,
"with hands as pale as milk.
"Lay them in gore,
"since you have shore
"with shears his thread of silk.
"Tongue, not a word.
"Come, trusty sword.
"Come, blade, my breast imbrue."

Thisby stabbed herself.

She continued, "And, farewell, friends.
"Thus Thisby ends.
"*Adieu, adieu, adieu.*"

She died.

"Moonshine and Lion are left to bury the dead," Theseus said.

"Yes, and Wall, too," Demetrius added.

The nobles' voices had gotten loud again.

Bottom heard the comments, came to life, and said, "No, I assure you; the Wall is down that separated their fathers. Will it please you to see the epilogue, or to hear a Bergomask dance between two of our company?"

"No epilogue, please, for your play needs no excuse," Theseus replied. "Never excuse; for when the players are all dead, there needs none to be blamed. Indeed, if he who wrote it had played Pyramus and hanged himself using Thisby's garter, it would have been a fine tragedy."

Hearing that there would be no epilogue, Quince and the remaining actors came onstage to rejoin Bottom and Thisby.

Theseus' jokes were funny, but cruel, and he stood for a moment and remembered that he had laughed hard during the play and that the play had done an excellent job of making the time pass quickly. Therefore, he added, "Your play is truly a fine tragedy, and all of you have *very notably discharged* it."

Theseus looked at Philostrate, and the look and his words were enough to communicate that these Athenian craftsmen would be rewarded monetarily for their intellectual and aesthetic labors.

Theseus then said, "No epilogue, please, but yes, most definitely we want to see your Bergomask dance."

The craftsmen danced, and then exited.

Afterwards, the craftsmen received the news of their monetary reward and made plans to meet together after work the following day to celebrate. At home, Quince thought about the audience reaction to his tragedy and reflected, *If the audience laughs at what is meant to be a deadly serious tragedy, wise actors — and a disappointed playwright — should say that they meant to make a comedy, not a tragedy. But wait! I did write a comedy — the word "comedy" even appears in the title: "The Most Lamentable Comedy, and Most Cruel Death of Pyramus and Thisby." The word "tragedy" does not appear in the title at all. The audience's laughter means that I am a successful writer of comedy, and all my friends are successful comedians. I can't wait to tell them tomorrow night!*

During the Bergomask dance, Theseus reflected that the craftsmen had done too well their job of helping to pass the time. Before the craftsmen's play, he had been eager for time to pass so that he could take Hippolyta to bed, but now — although he was still eager to take Hippolyta to bed — he discovered that everyone had stayed up past the time for the joys of bed to begin.

Theseus said, "The iron tongue of midnight has tolled twelve times on the clock. Lovers, all of us must go to bed — it is almost fairy time. I fear we shall sleep throughout the coming morning as much as we this night have stayed up too late. This obviously bad — but very funny — play has well helped us pass the slow hours until bedtime. Sweet friends, let us go to bed. Throughout the next two weeks, we will celebrate with nightly revelry and with new joys."

The humans exited.

Puck flew into the great chamber and said, "Now the hungry lion roars,

"and the wolf howls at the Moon,

"while the sleepy plowman snores,

"worn out by weary tasks too soon.

"Now the burned firebrands do glow,

"while the screech-owl, screeching loud,

"puts the wretch who lies in woe

"in remembrance of a shroud.

"Now it is the time of night

"when all the graves gape wide.

"Each one lets forth his sprite,

"in the churchway paths to glide.

"And we fairies, who do run

"by the Moon's dragon-team

"from the presence of the Sun,

"following darkness like a dream,

"now are merry. Not a mouse

"shall disturb this blessed house.

"I am sent with broom before,

"to sweep the dust behind the door."

As Puck spoke, he performed the job he traditionally did for good people: housework. (For lazy people, he made more work.)

Oberon and Titania flew into the great chamber with their attendant fairies.

Oberon said, "Through the house give gathering light,

"by the dead and drowsy fire.

"Every elf and fairy sprite

"hop as light as bird from brier;

"and this ditty, after me,

"sing, and dance it trippingly."

Titania said, "First, rehearse your song by rote

"to each word a warbling note.

"Hand in hand, with fairy grace,

"will we sing, and bless this place."

Oberon, Titania, and the other fairies sang and danced.

Oberon said, "Now, until the break of day,

"through this house each fairy stray.

"To the best bride-beds go we,

"which by us shall blessed be;

"and the babies there created

"ever shall be fortunate.

"So shall all the couples three

"ever true in loving be;
"and the blots of Nature's hand
"shall not in their babies stand.
"No mole, hare lip, or scar,
"or mark monstrous, such as are
"despised in nativity,
"shall upon their children be.
"With this field-dew consecrated,
"every fairy take his gait;
"and each separate chamber bless,
"through this palace, with sweet peace,
"so that the owner of it blest
"ever shall in safety rest.
"Trip away; make no stay.
"Meet me all by break of day."

Oberon, Titania, and the other fairies flew away, leaving only Puck. He knew that the bedsprings in various bedrooms were squeaking, and he wanted to have the last words in speaking:

"If we shadows have offended,
"think but this, and all is mended,
"that you have but slumbered here
"while these visions did appear.
"And this weak and idle theme
"has yielded nothing but a dream.
"Gentle people, do not reprehend.
"If you pardon, we will mend.
"And, as I am an honest Puck,
"if we have unearned luck
"now to escape the serpent's tongue

"that hisses thespians who lack pluck,
"we will make amends ere long,
"else the Puck a liar call.
"So, good night unto you all.
"Give me your hands, if we be friends.
"Applaud us during our curtain call,
"and Robin shall make amends."

AFTERWORD

The major theme of *A Midsummer Night's Dream* is love and the silly things it makes us do:

- Love can make us see a distinction where no real distinction exists. Lysander and Demetrius are very much alike, and Hermia and Helena are very much alike.
- Love can make us desire someone who is totally unsuitable for us. For a while, the fairy Queen, Titania, loves the ass-headed Bottom.
- Love can make us blind to the loved one's faults.
- Love can make us jealous.
- Love (and jealousy) can make friends enemies.
- Love can make us quarrelsome.
- Love can make us fickle.
- We can fall in and out of love very quickly, and we can love, then not love, and then love again the same person.
- If we are rejected, love can make us have low self-esteem. Helena has very low self-esteem for much of *A Midsummer Night's Dream*.
- Love can make us chase after someone who hates us.
- Love can make us attempt to use reason to explain love although love is a nonrational emotion. Lysander does this.
- Love is not irrational, although it can make people act in silly ways. Love is nonrational.
- If a tall woman steals your boyfriend, you may think that she was able to steal him because she is tall and you are short.

• One of the best comments on the nonrationality of love is made by Bottom: "And yet, to say the truth, reason / and love keep little company together nowadays."

Appendix A: About the Author

It was a dark and stormy night. Suddenly a cry rang out, and on a hot summer night in 1954, Josephine, wife of Carl Bruce, gave birth to a boy — me. Unfortunately, this young married couple allowed Reuben Saturday, Josephine's brother, to name their first-born. Reuben, aka "The Joker," decided that Bruce was a nice name, so he decided to name me Bruce Bruce. I have gone by my middle name — David — ever since.

Being named Bruce David Bruce hasn't been all bad. Bank tellers remember me very quickly, so I don't often have to show an ID. It can be fun in charades, also. When I was a counselor as a teenager at Camp Echoing Hills in Warsaw, Ohio, a fellow counselor gave the signs for "sounds like" and "two words," then she pointed to a bruise on her leg twice. Bruise Bruise? Oh yeah, Bruce Bruce is the answer!

Uncle Reuben, by the way, gave me a haircut when I was in kindergarten. He cut my hair short and shaved a small bald spot on the back of my head. My mother wouldn't let me go to school until the bald spot grew out again.

Of all my brothers and sisters (six in all), I am the only transplant to Athens, Ohio. I was born in Newark, Ohio, and have lived all around Southeastern Ohio. However, I moved to Athens to go to Ohio University and have never left.

At Ohio U, I never could make up my mind whether to major in English or Philosophy, so I got a bachelor's degree with a double major in both areas, then I added a master's degree in English and a master's degree in Philosophy.

Currently, and for a long time to come (I eat fruits and veggies), I am spending my retirement writing books such as *Nadia Comaneci: Perfect 10*, *The Funniest People in Dance*, *Homer's* Iliad: *A Retelling in Prose*, and *William Shakespeare's* Othello: *A Retelling in Prose*.

By the way, my sister Brenda Kennedy writes romances such as *A New Beginning* and *Shattered Dreams*.

Appendix B: Some Books by David Bruce

Retellings of a Classic Work of Literature

Arden of Faversham: *A Retelling*

Ben Jonson's The Alchemist: *A Retelling*

Ben Jonson's The Arraignment, or Poetaster: *A Retelling*

Ben Jonson's Bartholomew Fair: *A Retelling*

Ben Jonson's The Case is Altered: *A Retelling*

Ben Jonson's Catiline's Conspiracy: *A Retelling*

Ben Jonson's The Devil is an Ass: *A Retelling*

Ben Jonson's Epicene: *A Retelling*

Ben Jonson's Every Man in His Humor: *A Retelling*

Ben Jonson's Every Man Out of His Humor: *A Retelling*

Ben Jonson's The Fountain of Self-Love, or Cynthia's Revels: *A Retelling*

Ben Jonson's The Magnetic Lady, or Humors Reconciled: *A Retelling*

Ben Jonson's The New Inn, or The Light Heart: *A Retelling*

Ben Jonson's Sejanus' Fall: *A Retelling*

Ben Jonson's The Staple of News: *A Retelling*

Ben Jonson's A Tale of a Tub: *A Retelling*

Ben Jonson's Volpone, or the Fox: *A Retelling*

Christopher Marlowe's Complete Plays: Retellings

Christopher Marlowe's Dido, Queen of Carthage: *A Retelling*

Christopher Marlowe's Doctor Faustus: *Retellings of the 1604 A-Text and of the 1616 B-Text*

Christopher Marlowe's Edward II: *A Retelling*

Christopher Marlowe's The Massacre at Paris: *A Retelling*

Christopher Marlowe's The Rich Jew of Malta: *A Retelling*

Christopher Marlowe's Tamburlaine, Parts 1 and 2: *Retellings*

Dante's Divine Comedy: *A Retelling in Prose*

Dante's Inferno: *A Retelling in Prose*

Dante's Purgatory: *A Retelling in Prose*

Dante's Paradise: *A Retelling in Prose*

The Famous Victories of Henry V: *A Retelling*

From the Iliad *to the* Odyssey: *A Retelling in Prose of Quintus of Smyrna's* Posthomerica

George Chapman, Ben Jonson, and John Marston's Eastward Ho! *A Retelling*

George Peele's The Arraignment of Paris: *A Retelling*

George Peele's The Battle of Alcazar: *A Retelling*

George's Peele's David and Bathsheba, and the Tragedy of Absalom: *A Retelling*

George Peele's Edward I: *A Retelling*

George Peele's The Old Wives' Tale: *A Retelling*

George-a-Greene: *A Retelling*

The History of King Leir: *A Retelling*

Homer's Iliad: *A Retelling in Prose*

Homer's Odyssey: *A Retelling in Prose*

J.W. Gent.'s The Valiant Scot: *A Retelling*

Jason and the Argonauts: A Retelling in Prose of Apollonius of Rhodes' Argonautica

John Ford: Eight Plays Translated into Modern English

John Ford's The Broken Heart: *A Retelling*

John Ford's The Fancies, Chaste and Noble: *A Retelling*

John Ford's The Lady's Trial: *A Retelling*

John Ford's The Lover's Melancholy: *A Retelling*

John Ford's Love's Sacrifice: *A Retelling*

John Ford's Perkin Warbeck: *A Retelling*

John Ford's The Queen: *A Retelling*

John Ford's 'Tis Pity She's a Whore: *A Retelling*

John Lyly's Campaspe: *A Retelling*

John Lyly's Endymion, The Man in the Moon: *A Retelling*

John Lyly's Galatea: *A Retelling*

John Lyly's Love's Metamorphosis: *A Retelling*

John Lyly's Midas: *A Retelling*

John Lyly's Mother Bombie: *A Retelling*

John Lyly's Sappho and Phao: *A Retelling*

John Lyly's The Woman in the Moon: *A Retelling*

John Webster's The White Devil: *A Retelling*

King Edward III: *A Retelling*

Mankind: *A Medieval Morality Play* (A Retelling)

Margaret Cavendish's The Unnatural Tragedy: *A Retelling*

The Merry Devil of Edmonton: *A Retelling*

The Summoning of Everyman: *A Medieval Morality Play* (A Retelling)

Robert Greene's Friar Bacon and Friar Bungay: *A Retelling*

The Taming of a Shrew: *A Retelling*

Tarlton's Jests: A Retelling

Thomas Middleton's A Chaste Maid in Cheapside: *A Retelling*

Thomas Middleton's Women Beware Women: *A Retelling*

Thomas Middleton and Thomas Dekker's The Roaring Girl: *A Retelling*

Thomas Middleton and William Rowley's The Changeling: *A Retelling*

The Trojan War and Its Aftermath: Four Ancient Epic Poems

Virgil's Aeneid: *A Retelling in Prose*

William Shakespeare's 5 Late Romances: Retellings in Prose

William Shakespeare's 10 Histories: Retellings in Prose

William Shakespeare's 11 Tragedies: Retellings in Prose

William Shakespeare's 12 Comedies: Retellings in Prose

William Shakespeare's 38 Plays: Retellings in Prose

William Shakespeare's 1 Henry IV, aka Henry IV, Part 1: *A Retelling in Prose*

William Shakespeare's 2 Henry IV, aka Henry IV, Part 2: *A Retelling in Prose*

William Shakespeare's 1 Henry VI, aka Henry VI, Part 1: *A Retelling in Prose*

William Shakespeare's 2 Henry VI, aka Henry VI, Part 2: *A Retelling in Prose*

William Shakespeare's 3 Henry VI, aka Henry VI, Part 3: *A Retelling in Prose*

William Shakespeare's All's Well that Ends Well: *A Retelling in Prose*

William Shakespeare's Antony and Cleopatra: *A Retelling in Prose*

William Shakespeare's As You Like It: *A Retelling in Prose*

William Shakespeare's The Comedy of Errors: *A Retelling in Prose*

William Shakespeare's Coriolanus: *A Retelling in Prose*

William Shakespeare's Cymbeline: *A Retelling in Prose*

William Shakespeare's Hamlet: *A Retelling in Prose*

William Shakespeare's Henry V: *A Retelling in Prose*

William Shakespeare's Henry VIII: *A Retelling in Prose*
William Shakespeare's Julius Caesar: *A Retelling in Prose*
William Shakespeare's King John: *A Retelling in Prose*
William Shakespeare's King Lear: *A Retelling in Prose*
William Shakespeare's Love's Labor's Lost: *A Retelling in Prose*
William Shakespeare's Macbeth: *A Retelling in Prose*
William Shakespeare's Measure for Measure: *A Retelling in Prose*
William Shakespeare's The Merchant of Venice: *A Retelling in Prose*
William Shakespeare's The Merry Wives of Windsor: *A Retelling in Prose*
William Shakespeare's A Midsummer Night's Dream: *A Retelling in Prose*
William Shakespeare's Much Ado About Nothing: *A Retelling in Prose*
William Shakespeare's Othello: *A Retelling in Prose*
William Shakespeare's Pericles, Prince of Tyre: *A Retelling in Prose*
William Shakespeare's Richard II: *A Retelling in Prose*
William Shakespeare's Richard III: *A Retelling in Prose*
William Shakespeare's Romeo and Juliet: *A Retelling in Prose*
William Shakespeare's The Taming of the Shrew: *A Retelling in Prose*
William Shakespeare's The Tempest: *A Retelling in Prose*
William Shakespeare's Timon of Athens: *A Retelling in Prose*
William Shakespeare's Titus Andronicus: *A Retelling in Prose*
William Shakespeare's Troilus and Cressida: *A Retelling in Prose*
William Shakespeare's Twelfth Night: *A Retelling in Prose*
William Shakespeare's The Two Gentlemen of Verona: *A Retelling in Prose*
William Shakespeare's The Two Noble Kinsmen: *A Retelling in Prose*
William Shakespeare's The Winter's Tale: *A Retelling in Prose*